D1253003

VANISHING TRAILS

A SMOKY MOUNTAIN MYSTERY

RUTH MCCOY

VANISHING TRAILS

Copyright ©2023 by Smoky Mountain Mysteries

This book is a work of fiction. Names, characters, places, and incidents are the product of the author's imagination or are used fictitiously. Any resemblance to actual events, locales, or persons, living or dead, is coincidental.

All rights reserved. No part of this publication may be reproduced, distributed, or transmitted in any form or by any means, including photocopying, recording, or other electronic or mechanical methods, without the prior written permission of the publisher, except in the case of brief quotations embodied in critical reviews and certain other noncommercial uses permitted by copyright law.

For permission requests, contact Smoky Mountain Mysteries at TarheelLinda@gmail.com

ISBN: 9798987472125 (trade paperback)

Ruth McCoy is the pen name of Linda McCoy Cromartie

Cover Design and Formatting by The Book Khaleesi

Praise for Appalachian Trails: A Smoky Mountain Mystery

"I just finishedAppalachian Trails and wanted to tell you how much I enjoyed it. Well done! I like your main character, Daisy. I love her relationship with the stray cat - so endearing. You capture the mountains and flora beautifully, and I love how de Soto and the Cherokee add layers to the mystery. My one complaint is the salad recipe on page 99. I had a hard time concentrating after that it sounded so good."

~Sara Johnson, author of The Bone Track and other Alexa Glock mysteries

"This was a quick and easy read. Great for a day at the beach or on a plane or train ride. Daisy defiantly has the nothing scares me attitude a good investigating reporter needs, and Jake is the kind of guy we all wish we had on our side by our side. I enjoyed the history and the Franklin setting. I have a daughter who has lived there for a few years so that was fun too. I can't wait to see what is instore for Daisy and Jake next."

~Verified Amazon Reader

"This is a mystery reminiscent of Carolyn Keene, but with a grownup Nancy Drew who is a reporter in a small town in the mountains of North Carolina. Daisy uses her instincts, her hometown contacts, and her family and friends to help her doggedly pursue the story of a mysterious plane crash and its ties to the community. The author did a wonderful job with her setting of Franklin, NC, and the next time I'm close, plan to stop by and explore the town and the mountain toads surrounding. I look forward to Ms. McCoy's next book, as she develops her characters and their relationships further (including Rescue the cat!)"

~Verified Amazon Reader

"Too tame a mystery for Dashiell Hammett, though beyond Nancy Drew, this is an excellent mystery for mystery lovers. From the opening Cessna plane crash (and delayed explosion) to the conclusion Ruth McCoy has written a fun tale. Daisy keeps the plot moving with associated characters both living and dead introduced, and the reader cheers her on toward the plot's treasure."

~Verified Amazon Reader

"In this fine mystery, a newspaper reporter braves storms and threats to investigate a small plane crash on a mountain and perhaps learn why her mother died nearby years before. The author brings out the local color and characters, including the legend of Spanish explorer De Soto and a Cherokee princess."

~Verified Amazon Reader

Also by Ruth McCoy

Appalachian Trails: A Smoky Mountain Mystery

For Christopher and Katharine

Avoiding danger is no safer in the long run than outright exposure. The fearful are caught as often as the bold. Faith alone defends. Life is either a daring adventure or nothing. To keep our faces toward change and behave like free spirits in the presence of fate is strength undefeatable.

~ **Helen Keller, The Open Door**

PROLOGUE

When we closed on our house in Franklin, North Carolina, our agent took me aside to tell me how to pronounce Cartoogechaye. Important to know as it is the name of our area, the creek that runs through it, and the local elementary school.

"If you say *Cart-ogg-eee-cha-yeah*, natives and long-time residents can immediately tell that you have not belonged here long. Say *Car-too-gah-chay* with the primary accent on *too* and secondary on *chay*."

Simple enough. I think of it as the sound a train would make if you repeatedly say it fast.

Another important landmark is the Cullaseja Gorge with its impressive falls that is a must see for tourist brave enough to take the road that twists and turns nightmarishly close to the edge between Franklin and Highlands. Not *Cull-ah-see-hah*, as the uninitiated might venture a guess but *Coo-luh-say-jah*.

This arcane information will not make the mysteries set in these ridges and valleys of Southern Appalachia more enjoyable. Pronounce the words as the locals do or as the tourists do, and the story will not suffer. The same killings, kidnappings, drug smuggling, and, in the case of methamphetamines, drug production will still weave into the stories.

One word mispronounced will make a difference as to how one of the characters is perceived, and that name is *Louisa*. If you think of the well-known writers Louisa May Alcott or Louise Penny, you are on the wrong track. Never a popular name in literature, Louisa Hurst is one of the snobbish sisters who try to undermine Elizabeth Bennet in *Pride and Prejudice*. Small wonder it is not used often by authors.

Low-wise-ah with the stress on the second syllable is how to pronounce her name, the Louisa Chapel Road, and the Louisa Chapel, itself a United Methodist Church in Macon County; however, this Louisa, as the local pronunciation suggests, was not born into a cultured family, but what she lacks in culture she more than makes up in enthusiasm.

CHAPTER

1

Daisy McLaren had needed time and therapy to come to grips with the fact that she had killed and had almost been killed last fall. A spring semester in Chapel Hill provided the distance she needed to recover. Believing her feet were planted on solid ground and lightning never struck the same place twice also helped. Now she was back in Franklin, living in the apartment over her father's garage, but questions remained.

How could I have been so reckless? If I'd waited for help, Jake would not have been shot, and I wouldn't have killed Walker and his son. Why had Jasmine Walker killed Christian just as he was explaining why he was threatening her? And most of all, why had Keira disappeared and where could she be?

She had grown closer to Jake, and they had talked about going somewhere for the Fourth of July weekend. She had arranged to take extra days off to make it long, but with a forecast of rain, they stayed put to celebrate the holiday in Franklin. Weather permitting, they would pick the first blackberries of the season.

Now she was content to sit reading and occasionally petting Rescue. A knock on the door interrupted, and she looked out to see Ed, her father's chef and all-around assistant.

"Cat-sitter reporting for duty."

Ed grinned as Rescue rushed over and climbed up his leg to snuggle against his chest. "How's my little buddy today?" he said, as he vigorously rubbed the calico. Ed insisted on treating the petite female as he would a dog. Daisy could never figure out the reason why Rescue loved it.

"I've got everything ready, a box with clean litter, salmon Friskies as a treat, new toys," Daisy said.

"That's fine, Daisy, but I'm going to take her back to Lucas's and we've already got all that stuff over there. Seemed like too much trouble to have to cart everything back and forth every time she needed to stay over. Besides, she likes to play with Stripey."

Stripey was the only male in Rescue's surprise litter, delivered before Daisy could have the calico spayed. He was a large gray tabby. Jake took a female orange tabby, and the other kitten went home with Maxie who managed Lucas's law office.

"I'm only away for one night!"

"Just in case, Daisy. Just in case."

"You ready, pal?" he asked the cat.

"See you tomorrow night," he said as he stepped back outside with Rescue.

"Meewrow," the cat said as a farewell to Daisy.

"I guess that's that," Daisy said to herself. She went to her closet for an overnight bag, packed it with a few essentials, and left the apartment.

Light clouds filled the sky on a typical summer day in the mountains, warm but not too hot, temperature in the low eighties. Heavy rains were forecast but would not arrive until early evening or overnight. She and Jake would have plenty of time to pick blackberries.

She stopped by the BP to fill up her red Jeep and to buy a Coke, as was her habit. Traffic was light on the highway, and she soon reached the exit that would take her to Wayah Road. A usual crowd of biker retirees had gathered in front of Loafer's Glory before taking off to ride the "Dragon's Tail," the zigzagged road along a cliff face on the route to Nantahala. She was glad to get ahead of the pack.

On Wayah Road she drove through alternating pastures and woodlands. Kudzu--which some well-intentioned person brought in to stop erosion, or where some innocent bird dropped seeds in its feces—kudzu vines had taken over the woods and now the dormant vines were being revived to drape the trees and brush with greenery.

The motorcycle riding club was fast catching up with Daisy. She sped up a little and was relieved when she turned, quickly and sharply, into the Smiths' long driveway to their farm. She stopped to catch her breath before moving down the road. Blackberry canes hung vines heavy with plump, black fruit over the road. They tempted her to linger and feast, but knowing Jake and Clemmie were expecting her, she drove on.

She parked in front of the house where Jake lived with his mother. Clemmie Smith had relied on her son to keep the farm going since his father abandoned them when Jake was a teen. Jake worked full-time at Drake Enterprises with the understanding that he could go out when the *Franklin Free Press* called on him for photography. That Daisy worked there as a reporter was a plus. He kept those jobs mainly to cover regular expenses.

He had made a lot of money from *Appalachian Trails*, a role-playing game he had created. It was based on the valley, the mountains, and life as it was in the early twentieth century. He kept that money in a savings account. Jake was a practical man with big dreams.

The house was a typical two-story North Carolina farmhouse, L-shaped with a kitchen extension and porches on front and back. The back porch had a shed roof and was screened in. Daisy walked around to enter this porch and from there to enter the kitchen.

"Jake, Clemmie," Daisy called out as she let herself in. She was surprised to receive no reply.

CHAPTER

2

Daisy set her overnight bag by the door and went back out. Blackberries grew along the edges of land left for pasture and in clumps throughout this untended area, not in the garden where she and Jake usually worked, but Daisy thought she remembered the way. She walked to the other side of the yard, where she saw another path through the hedge.

Jake and his mother were at the other end of the path. They were almost finished with gathering blackberries and were fixing to carry them to the house. Suzie Q, Jake's Redbone hound, was lying in the shade of a big oak and jumped up to greet Daisy.

"Need any help? It looks like you two have this under control." Daisy laughed as she scratched the hound's head.

"You took your own sweet time getting here, darlin', but it's your lucky day. We've saved a plenty for you."

Jake handed Daisy a shallow basket. She spotted a bush likely to hold ripe fruit and began to pick only fully-ripened berries. She learned long ago that the ripe ones left the vine easily. No need to tug. No pressure was needed, thus ensuring the berries would not be crushed. She had not brought a water bottle along, but eating ripe berries kept her thirst sated. Nothing juicier than a plump berry eaten in the field.

It was not long before Daisy finished for the day. Jake had waited for her. "Got something I want to show you, Daisy. Come this way."

He took her hand and walked to a path that led to an area between the two gardens. Suzie Q followed close behind, stopping occasionally to explore and put her own mark on various wildlife scents. They soon reached another section where the woods and shrubs had been cleared. Daisy could see the farmhouse over the hedge separating the clearing from the house.

"What's this?"

"A surprise. Been working on this all spring. After the Fourth I've got a crew coming in to put in a well and septic, already permitted. The following week a kit for building a log cabin should be delivered. I can show you the plans later."

"You're building a house?" Daisy was amazed. "But why?"

"Look darlin', I like living on the farm and being able to help Mom, but I'm ready to be on my own too. This way I get the best of both worlds."

"All I can say is you certainly are better at keeping a secret than I thought you'd be. I remember when you ratted me out when I'd planned to go to Atlanta for a weekend. You went and told Mom there wasn't any cheerleading competition that weekend."

"That was for your own good."

"I think you were just jealous, afraid Ted Siler and I would get together." Daisy's eyes twinkled.

"Seriously?"

"Well, he *was* the quarterback." She paused to get the full effect. "And he was awful good-looking."

"Stop it! Mom's waiting for us."

They went back to the house, where Clemmie waited with the blackberries. "Not bad for a day's work. Let's get these to the kitchen."

"Do you want us to start on these now?" Jake asked.

"They can rest 'til morning. I've covered them with paper towels and put them in the other refrigerator. Supper won't be ready for a while. Having leftovers."

"Do we have time for a walk?" Jake asked.

"If you hurry."

Jake took Daisy's hand. "Let's go."

Several hours remained until dusk, but fast-moving clouds were already darkening the sky. The first heavy drops were a prelude to the promised downpour to follow in the evening. In the distance, clouds glowed white, holding the lightning's power at bay. A low rumbling increased to a roar like the drumming of timpani in a symphony resounding across the valley.

Daisy and Jake continued their walk, with Suzie Q at

heel, toward the low bridge that led to the other side of Wayah Creek. When Jake stopped to embrace her, they gently kissed.

"I hope you're here for good this time," Jake said. "Franklin wasn't the same without you."

"I had to get away. You know I thought about staying in Chapel Hill and getting my Master's. I could've worked there and reported on local news for the *N&O* but, when push came to shove, I realized I missed it here, the town, Dad, and everyone."

"You must mean me, darlin," Jake said with sparkling eyes. He put one arm around Daisy's shoulder and squeezed it. Before Daisy could make an appropriate retort, lightning sizzled across the sky soon followed by a jagged spear from cloud to ground. The grumbling thunder was replaced by a deafening boom that threatened to crack the sky open to let the rain pour down. They turned back to run, hand-in-hand, toward the house. Suzie Q raced ahead of them to wait on the front porch.

An exhausted Daisy begged off from supper, changed for bed, but she could not fall asleep. A fierce storm raged outside. Thoughts of Jake, which should make her happy, created a knot in her stomach. Clearly Jake loved her, and she loved Jake, but she was not able to trust him completely. Until she shared with him what had happened to her in Chapel Hill, that would not change.

Maybe I'll tell him tomorrow.

CHAPTER

3

A gentle rain pattered against the window when Daisy awoke the following morning in the Smith's guest room. She held the covers close under her chin and looked around the cozy room. A mix of wildflowers in a pottery vase, a glass, and small pitcher of water on the nightstand, and fresh towels atop the antique oak chest of drawers brought a smile to Daisy's face. She appreciated the feminine touches Clemmie provided, extras that were frequently neglected in her room at Lucas's, since her mother died. A white terrycloth robe hung on the back of the door. Daisy put it on and walked to the kitchen.

Clemmie was at the stove, stirring a large pot. The fragrance told Daisy that the jam was already simmering. Jake was nowhere to be seen.

"Don't tell me you've done all this by yourself."

"Good morning, dear," Clemmie greeted her. "No, Jake

helped me, and this part is easy. I thought you needed more rest and it's always nice to sleep in on rainy mornings."

"Thank you. I think you're right. What time is it?"

Clemmie glanced at the wall clock.

"Almost noon."

"Where's Jake?"

"Went to get fireworks for us to use tonight. The town might go on with their show, but he decided we would skip that," she said. "There's coffee made."

Daisy poured herself a mug and stepped onto the porch. Ambrosia, the orange tabby Jake had chosen from Rescue's litter, lounged in a rocking chair.

"I guess Suzie Q went with Jake."

"You guessed right. He should've called her Shadow. Dogs his steps everywhere. Daddy's girl."

As if on cue, Jake's Dodge Ram roared into the back yard. Suzie Q jumped through an open window and ran with wagging tail to Daisy. Ambrosia dashed to safety under the porch. The rain was now pouring down, and the dog shook off raindrops and shimmied as Daisy rubbed behind her ears. Jake came running with a paper bag.

"Think you bought enough fireworks?'

"Probably not, but these will have to do," Jake said as he put an arm around Daisy and bent over to kiss her.

Daisy went to shower and dress for the day. Seeing Jake gave her second thoughts about trying to have a serious talk about her past in Chapel Hill with him. After all, it was a holiday.

When Daisy returned to the kitchen, Jake was sitting at the

kitchen table and sorting the fireworks. North Carolina law did not permit any that would be considered exciting. None could explode, launch into the air, or even twirl around.

He laid out several boxes of sparklers and a $19.97 box of assorted fireworks with several fountains of assorted sizes, poppers, snakes that would add a lot of smoke but no lights. The names—Rose Blossom, Golden Shower, and Lightning Flash—promised more than they could possibly deliver. Groans and jokes would provide a lot of the night's entertainment about the uninspired display.

"D'you think we'll be able to cook out tonight?" Jake asked his mother.

"Don't know, but we can do the hot dogs and burgers inside. Slaw and potato salad are in the refrigerator. Might have to keep watermelon for another day."

"Can I help with something?" Daisy asked.

"No, dear. You just take a load off."

Daisy thought she could enjoy Clemmie's mothering.

The phone rang and Clemmie said, "Now who could that be?"

She answered and handed the phone to Daisy. It was Lexie.

"Daisy, I thought you should know. Keira just turned up on our doorstep."

"Keira Swan?"

Jake and his mother stopped what they were doing and looked with interest at Daisy.

"Yes, and you won't believe this—she has a baby."

"A baby! Is it hers?"

"I think so. I don't know why she'd have it otherwise. I've got to go, but I knew you were so worried about Keira."

"Thanks. Can I come by tomorrow?"

"Sure thing."

Daisy hung up the phone and turned to fill in the details.

"I guess you heard, Keira is back, and she has a baby with her."

They were all at a loss for words at this revelation.

"What do you make of Keira coming back to Franklin with a baby?"

Daisy started the conversation about the young girl who was on everyone's mind.

Jake simply shook his head and looked down.

"I understand why she went to Lexie instead of her family," Clemmie said. "They were never much use to her."

"I don't think I know the Swans," Daisy said.

"You wouldn't. They've always been ne'er-do-wells, not criminals, but right on the edge. They claimed to homeschool their children but stopped pretending when the kids reached sixteen.

"This current bunch is the worst. They still make moonshine. But they've also been picked up for peddling drugs and guns. And other things I don't care to talk about."

Daisy did not push the point as she respected Clemmie too much to argue.

"But Keira was very bright. Lexie and Brad thought a lot of her when she worked at their bookstore. I guess I'll learn more when I go see them tomorrow."

She sat in silence, absent-mindedly stroking the orange tabby who had jumped on her lap and turning thoughts over in her mind, until finally Jake got up and said, "Do you want to look at the plans for the cabin?"

Daisy nodded. "If you really don't need my help, Clemmie."

In the living room, Jake had spread out the plans with several drawings. The log cabin had two levels. Essentially an A-frame with a wrap-around porch, most of the rooms were on the first level, but there was a bedroom suite upstairs with an additional loft that could remain open to below or enclosed.

"I'm planning to shut off the loft for privacy."

Daisy laughed. "Privacy from who? Suzie Q?"

"Go ahead and laugh, darlin'. He who laughs last..."

He picked up one of the drawings and pointed out the small, covered porch on the left.

"That's the main entrance. I'm going to enclose it to make a mudroom."

Then he pointed out a shed roof covering part of the wrap-around porch on the other side.

"And this will be the screen porch. With plenty of room for rocking chairs and a glider."

Daisy smiled to think he was honoring her parents with this. She had spent many mornings and evenings with them on a porch just like that—and many nights making out with Jake on the glider. She could not think how to change this moment so that she could tease Jake. Things were happening fast. She could tell Jake was including her in his plans for the house, but she was not able to make that commitment now. Maybe never.

She felt her heart beginning to race, signaling an impending panic attack. She took a deep breath and held it, released it, and repeated. She calmed herself until she could say, "It actually looks nice. Building it will keep you off the streets for quite a while."

"Clearing the land was the hard part. I'm hiring a few guys from the fire department to help. It should be completed by fall. Maybe you can help me pick out furniture and stuff."

"If you really need my help. You know you can order online from High Point and have it delivered."

Jake nodded. They looked at the log cabin plans a bit longer and then returned to the kitchen.

CHAPTER

4

By evening there was a lull in the rain, and they could cook burgers and hot dogs on the barbecue grill. The fireworks display sizzled and smoked as expected and elicited many growls and woofs from Suzie Q, who hung behind Jake all evening.

After supper Daisy cleaned the grill rack, while Jake helped his mother lift the heavy canning rack that held sealed jars of blackberry jam from a bath of boiling water. Then she went inside to get her things.

"Sure you have to go?" Jake asked.

"Yep, I've got to go to Lexie's and, before I do, I want to ask Lucas if he knows any more about Keira and her family." She added, "I get more from him if I ask face to face so he can't weasel out."

Daisy had assumed Keira was dead when she suddenly disappeared last November. She had contacted various social service departments for updates through the winter and finally gave up. Keira had either been kidnapped or she had taken some of the heroin that killed Joe Taylor. Daisy had believed Keira would have contacted Lexie if she could have, so it followed that she must have died.

Now another possibility emerged. Keira became pregnant and wanted to go somewhere else to have the baby. But why? Unwed mothers were not shunned in Franklin. Shotgun weddings still existed, although it did not sound as though the Swans would have insisted on *any* kind of wedding.

Who was the father? Did he make it impossible for Keira to stay in Franklin? Could she have been raped?

CHAPTER

5

As Daisy drove along Wayah Road and then on the two-lane Old Murphy Highway back to town, question after question filled her mind, and she could not get answers to any until she spoke with Keira in the morning. Tonight she would rely on Lucas for background information.

When she entered the large kitchen, the first thing she saw was Rescue. Daisy was not surprised when the petite calico decided to ignore her. Some form of punishment followed any prolonged absence that seemed like desertion. Never mind that Rescue adored Ed and Lucas. The point the cat made was that Daisy was her human and as such had a great responsibility.

"At least you didn't tear the place up."

At last Rescue allowed Daisy to pick her up and began to purr as she nestled into Daisy's chest. Lucas came onto the scene walking without a cane. The months of therapy provided by Ed had returned strength lost when he developed Post-Polio Syndrome. During those months Ed had become a permanent resident and member of the family.

"She's welcome to stay."

Daisy laughed and set the cat down.

"I'd never hear the end of it if I left her overnight again. Where's Stripey?"

On cue the lanky adolescent tabby struck from beneath the table and pounced on his mother who promptly flipped over, grabbed his head with her front paws, and scratched violently at him with her hind claws. Daisy and Lucas let them be. They knew they were only play-fighting and that neither would end up with a serious bite or scratch that could turn into an abscess.

Daisy hugged her father and said, "Actually I need to talk to you. About the Swan family, and Keira."

Lucas raised his eyebrows, and Daisy continued, "She showed up at Lexie and Brad's yesterday—with a baby."

"Well, that's quite a development. Did she say where she'd been keeping herself?"

"I haven't talked to her yet. I'm going out there in the morning. I know her family didn't work and probably made their living by stealing, pushing drugs, and lord knows what else. Keira was an outlier. I really thought she was dead until now."

Daisy opened the refrigerator and got a Coke, popped it open, and drank from the can.

"I just can't understand why Keira felt she had to leave Franklin when she became pregnant. No one here would have been bothered by that. Do you know anything else about the family? Would they have threatened or harmed her?"

"I don't think they'd have the energy to do that. Aside from criminal activities, they didn't do much. In my opinion, they probably forgot Keira was there, and Keira seemed to spend most of her time away from that house. When she wasn't at school, she studied with friends at the library."

"And she had the job at the bookstore," Daisy said.

"Yes, I believe she only went home to sleep."

Daisy drank the last of the Coke. She kissed Lucas and picked Rescue up.

"See you tomorrow."

"I know you want to find out what's happened, but please—let Ben look into it."

Daisy nodded over her shoulder and stepped out into the storm which was pelting the ground and Daisy with hard drops of rain. She pulled Rescue tight against her chest, bent over her, and ran across the driveway to the stairs to her garage apartment.

Once inside she released Rescue and went to her room where she changed into a clean t-shirt and a favorite cozy chenille robe. She returned to the kitchen to make a cup of chamomile tea. The cat was meowing in frustration and placed her paws on the wall under the window that faced the woods behind the garage.

The cold front that ushered in the rain also lowered the temperature. Daisy opened the window for her cat. Rescue immediately jumped onto the sill to listen to night sounds and watch over the woods out back. Her ears flicked at each rustle of leaves or croak of the bullfrogs.

Daisy chose a book and stretched out with her tea on the couch to read, but images of Keira raced through her thoughts until overtaken by flashbacks of the events last fall at the Franklin airport. She shook herself out of it to consider the next day when she would ask Keira what had happened. No reasonable explanation came to mind.

Carrying the book to her room, she got ready for bed. By the time she had finished brushing her teeth and using cold cream to clean her face, the little calico had already assumed her place on the pillow. A sky-blue journal and several pens in a chipped crystal water glass were ready on the bedside table. Journaling had become almost a nightly ritual since the previous November when she returned to therapy with Dr. Ammons. The psychiatrist gave her the first notebook to use. Daisy was on her third.

"Keira is alive!" she wrote. "She is at Lexie's, and she has brought an infant that she says is her own. I can see her in the morning, and I'm looking forward to hearing her story. But I also dread it. I can feel my anxiety building, and I can't afford to lose control again. The breathing exercises help, but I'd rather not have panic attacks to begin with.

"I'll make an appointment with Dr. Ammons.

"She'll want to talk about Mom, Chapel Hill, and all. I'd rather not but I know I've got to. I can't keep going around in circles. I need to find the courage to talk to Daddy and Jake about all that. Feeling like the Cowardly Lion tonight.

"Jake is building a house.

"More to come later."

After turning the bedside lamp off, she got under the covers and lay on her back. Thoughts of Keira alone in the world with a baby filled her mind. *Breathe in. Hold. Breathe out. Breathe in. Hold. Breathe out.* Why had she returned and chosen to see Lexie and Brad? She had worked in their bookstore, but still, they were not family. *Breathe in. Hold. Breathe out.* She continued until, relaxed, the anxiety was gone. She turned on her side to sleep. Rescue slid in beside her and settled in the crook of her legs.

CHAPTER

6

Midsummer mornings began the same way whether it had rained the previous day or not. A thick haze blurred the black outlines of trees and mountains under the dove gray sky that hung over the Smokies until the first rays of the sun peeked over the ridges.

By the time a bleary-eyed Daisy McLaren woke up, the early sun had climbed high enough to dry the air and cast golden streaks on the brown bark of the oaks behind her apartment. The activities of the previous days had sapped her energy, and she considered pulling the covers over her head and going back to sleep. The news about Keira's return had caused more stress than the physical labor on Jake's farm, and she was now not as eager to see and question her as she had been.

As she realized that Rescue was not in her usual spot under the covers, she got out of bed and went to the great room that served as living room and kitchen. The petite calico sat on the windowsill and focused her attention on the birds flitting and squirrels leaping among the trees. She ignored Daisy's call.

Daisy popped two pieces of whole wheat bread in the toaster slots and set up her Keurig to brew a cup of coffee. When she opened a can of cat food, Rescue rushed to entwine herself around Daisy's ankles.

"So, Rescue, you're just using me, huh?"

Rescue whined a meow. Daisy filled her bowl and placed it on the floor. The cat settled down to eat. As usual Daisy took her breakfast to the couch and turned on the television to find the morning's news. Having missed the broadcast from WLOS, the Asheville station that served Western North Carolina, she tuned in CNN.

The weather dominated the national news. On the west coast forest fires burned out of control. People were losing their homes and, in too many cases, their lives. Daisy could not imagine the forests covering the mountain ridges as charred shadows of themselves, or the wildlife trying to flee a horrible fate.

Global warming was cited as the cause of the extreme heat and the fires. The Appalachians experienced a drought several years ago. Lightning created fires on the ridges, but they were soon contained by wildland firefighters hired by the Forestry Service.

Temperatures at 3500 feet and higher trail the Piedmont by a good ten degrees. The valley where Franklin is situated seems to have its own weather that is moderate for most of the year.

Springs feed the many creeks and rivers that flow into

the Little Tennessee, then to the Tennessee River, once called the Cherokee River because of the many Cherokee tribes that settled along its banks. The Tennessee goes on to join the mighty Ohio. The dense carpet of leaves in the shaded woodlands retained moisture long after the storms passed.

Rescue disappeared into the bedroom. Daisy put the breakfast dishes in the sink and went to dress for the day. Upon returning to the great room, she saw her cat perched again on the windowsill.

"Guard the house, Rescue. Don't let any squirrels get close."

She bypassed Lucas's house and climbed into the red Jeep Compass Sport that her father bought for her when she crashed her old Jeep on Ruby Mine Road last November. She had decided to drive directly to see Keira.

The meadows of grass and alfalfa that farmers would mow for hay in the fall were a rich green. Vast cornfields held ripe ears, and migrant workers, who had finished setting out tomato plants in the spring, moved steadily through, picking choice ears. The remaining ears would be left to dry for the autumn harvest as animal feed.

She soon reached the exit for Wayah Road and stopped by Loafer's Glory for her morning Coke. Several touring motorcycles waited in the lot for the rest of their group to arrive. Riding primarily BMWs and Hondas, many retirees had exchanged their SUVs for the high-end bikes and often met there to meet the challenge offered by the Dragon's Tail on the way to Bryson City.

Daisy knew the manager's daughter who worked behind the counter. Maria Perez was a student at Appalachian State and, home for the summer, helped her parents in the small convenience store. She and Daisy had become friends over those summers. Daisy got a Coke and Nabs and went to pay.

"Maria, you must have graduated this year."

"I'm so excited. You know I got my B.A. in Creative Writing, and this fall I'll start working on my Master's in Chapel Hill. I got a fellowship, so I'll be teaching freshman English."

"I'm not surprised, Maria, but that's amazing."

"Yes, I'll be leaving in a few weeks—at the beginning of August."

"I'm sure I'll see you again before you leave."

Daisy paid for her snack and a newspaper and left. She thought of the difference between Maria's life and Keira's. Maria had a family that valued education and strove for their children to have all the advantages offered in North Carolina. The rules they set for their children were considered overly strict by Maria's friends, but in the end, the rules kept her on a path that led to graduation from high school and college, and now to the fellowship at UNC.

Keira's family thought only of how they could get by while doing as little as possible, even if the proceeds of petty crime paid their way. Keira had been different from them. She worked hard at school and at her job at the bookstore's café and had seemed on track to get a scholarship to community college or perhaps even to a state university. But then she had disappeared, and now here she was, with a baby in tow.

With her mind atwirl, Daisy almost drove by her destination. She turned sharply at the last second into the farm road. Fresh gravel had been added during June and the farmhouse had been completed over the winter. This was Daisy's first visit since last fall. She was more excited about seeing the house than seeing Keira, but it was necessary that she hear Keira's story and determine if it contained any clues about her mother's death during Daisy's last semester at Chapel Hill.

She parked her red Jeep between the stable and the house. She remained in the vehicle to consider how she would approach Keira. A severe, accusatory manner might alienate Keira, and she needed Keira's cooperation to get more information that might help her solve the mystery of her mother's death. Alice McLaren, a social worker, had been investigating the disappearances of young girls like Keira.

Getting out of the Sport, Daisy took several deep breaths, relaxed her facial muscles, and walked to the front door. Lexie opened it before she could knock. Daisy heard a baby bawling.

"She's gone! Keira's gone."

Dumbfounded, Daisy threw up her hands.

"But I hear the baby."

"She left it. Keira left her baby and has gone."

Lexie led her into the kitchen where Brad was attempting to coax the nipple of a baby bottle into the infant's mouth. By scrunching its eyes tight and clenching its lips in between wails, the tiny babe emphasized its refusal to nurse. Lexie took over with no success and eventually the poor baby cried itself to sleep. Daisy looked on all the while and tried to absorb what had happened.

"Did she leave a note to explain?"

"No note. Just a diaper bag with formula and these bottles."

Lexie motioned toward the counter where several plastic bottles with tops, a box of plastic bottle liners, and a can of formula were lined up. Daisy saw a pack of Pampers for Newborns and a box of wipes on the kitchen table.

"We heard the baby in the middle of the night, and when we didn't hear Keira tending to her, we went in. Keira was nowhere to be found."

Brad had made coffee and toast. He had laid places with hot coffee for Daisy and Lexie, so they joined him.

Daisy began, "What are you going to do?"

"We honestly have no idea," Lexie answered. "We haven't had time to think."

"First thing is a trip to Walmart," Brad, ever practical, said. "Pretty sure we'll need more diapers."

"I'm going to call Dr. Malone," Lexie added.

Dr. Malone had been Daisy's pediatrician.

"Maybe she can help us figure out the next steps."

"You'll have to notify Social Services," Daisy paused. "I could go by on my way to the office tomorrow."

"That would be a big help," Lexie said. "Why do you think she abandoned her baby?"

"It's not like she left it just anywhere," Daisy said. "She obviously trusts you to care for it. By the way, is it a boy or a girl?"

"A girl," Lexie said. "She named her Alexa, little Lexie."

Daisy was silent. It had become increasingly obvious that Keira had not simply left her baby with Lexie and Brad. She had entrusted her child to them. But why had she left?

What could Keira fear so much that she would leave her baby whom she clearly loved? Where had she been all this time?

Daisy would find out. First, she would help them get Alexa settled somewhere safe. Then she would get the answers to the questions Keira had left unanswered.

Keira's abrupt disappearance had wrecked Daisy's plans for the day. She thought of confronting Keira's family to see if they had a hand in this but realized that Keira would not have even let them know she had returned to Franklin. Instead, she drove on down Wayah Road to Jake's farm.

CHAPTER

7

S uzie Q ran from behind the house and Jake followed. "I didn't expect to see you this morning."

"I know, but Keira has disappeared again."

"With her baby?"

Daisy shook her head slowly.

"What happened?"

"Brad and Lexie don't know. She sneaked out in the middle of the night. I don't know what to do."

"Maybe Suzie Q can find her."

"How?"

"Well, I didn't need her to track and tree coons, like she's bred to do, so I started training her to follow trails left by people. I figured she could help find hikers lost in the mountains. A guy from work came by to help. She's still young—and flighty, but she's got a good nose, and she loves to play."

"Can't hurt, I guess. Can we go now?"

"Sure thing, darlin'. I just need to tell Mama. Meet you out front."

Suzie Q followed him into the house and soon they both came out the front door. Jake held a leash and a baggie.

"Liver snacks. A real reward for her."

After they explained what they were going to try, Lexie brought out the small blanket Keira's baby had been swaddled in.

"It'll have her scent as well as little Alexa's."

Lexie stayed with the baby as the others went outside. Jake put a harness on Suzie Q and attached the leash. The Redbone shimmied and pranced with excitement.

"I think we should drive out to Wayah Road to see if she can pick up her scent there. There won't be so many other scents, rabbit or coon, to distract her."

They piled in Daisy's red Jeep, left it at the end of the long driveway, and walked to the road. Jake stooped low by his dog and held out the blanket for her to smell.

"Are you ready to play?"

The Redbone wiggled her rump and wagged her tail excitedly. Jake gave her a liver snack.

"Okay, Suzie Q, go find!"

Jake maintained control with the leash as the hound with nose and ears to the ground ranged back and forth on the paved road. They had gone only a short distance when she let out a long howl and pleaded with her eyes for Jake to follow.

"Suzie Q, come. Sit! Still wiggling she promptly obeyed

and received another treat."

Jake unhooked the leash and gave the command, "Go find!"

Baying loudly as she ran, Suzie Q bounded down the road. She let out several howls punctuated with woofs and circled a spot in the distance.

Jake ran to her and commanded her again to sit. He gave her a treat as she sat, still looking around anxiously. She was not used to losing a trail.

"What's wrong, girl? Want to try again?"

He held the blanket to her nose and said, "Go find."

When Suzie Q started to backtrack, Jake recalled her and put her on the leash.

"Good girl," he said as he rubbed her behind the ears and gave her another liver snack. "Let's go home."

When he reached Daisy and the others, he said, "The only thing I can figure is that someone picked her up. In a car. The scent vanished."

They drove quietly back to Jake's farm. The events of the day so far added only more confusion and questions about Keira and her disappearances. Daisy knew that she would have to learn more about Keira's family, even visit them. She wanted to know if Keira had interacted with them at all during the time she was missing. But she took their nasty reputation seriously and decided to learn as much as she could, before approaching them.

Jake could probably tell her a lot, but he would also tell her to keep away. No, she would ask her father, Lucas. As a lawyer he would definitely know details about encounters with law enforcement and possibly about skirmishes with their neighbors. Sheriff Ben Williams had not been in town long enough to know their history, but Maxie who ran the office was always a reliable source for local gossip, behind the scenes information. That would be her second stop. Her strategy in place, Daisy enjoyed the rest of the day working in the garden with Jake until dark when they returned to Jake's house.

After dinner, Daisy went to the guest room and, exhausted, fell into bed. Her dreams held scenes of laurel thickets and kudzu vines. Keira appeared briefly holding her baby before disappearing into the tangled woods.

CHAPTER

8

Daisy woke early, quietly dressed, and headed toward home. In the east, the sun gleamed in a streak of silver above the ridge and below the scattered clouds. A bright day ahead.

She wanted to learn if Maria had heard anything in the neighborhood gossip, but Loafer's Glory was still closed. News traveled fast in the valley because of gathering spots like this, and the disappearance of a young woman was news in the tight-knit community along Wayah Road.

Eager to learn the reason for Keira's secretive disappearance, she went directly to Lucas's kitchen. Rescue heard the door opening and raced to leap onto the counter where Daisy was fixing a cup of leftover coffee to heat in the microwave.

"What are you doing, cat? Did you miss me?"

The small cat meowed in response and pushed her

head into Daisy's arm.

"Thought we had a burglar," Ed said as he entered the kitchen. Wrapped in a dingy bathrobe he tried to smooth his hair over his receding hairline. Too early for much vanity.

"Sorry Ed, I was trying to be quiet so I wouldn't wake anyone up. Guess you've been spoiling this cat."

"Didn't want her to get lonesome." He wagged his finger at the cat. "What did I say about countertops, 'Cue? Down!"

The calico immediately jumped down and wound in and out between Ed's ankles.

"A nickname? Seriously? Let's get you out of here before they start bathing you or something."

She picked the cat up.

"You can have the coffee, Ed. Tell Dad I need to talk to him."

Ed chuckled as the screen door slammed behind Daisy and her cat.

Back in her apartment over the garage, Daisy went to her small oak desk and opened her laptop. She had decided to write a brief notice about Keira to ask people to contact her or the sheriff if they had seen her or had any information. When she finished writing, she did a quick proofread and emailed it to Chad, the editor of the *Franklin Free Press*. She might be reaching for straws, but she would welcome any help.

Preparing for bed, she pulled on a t-shirt. In the bathroom, she brushed her teeth and then cleansed her face with Pond's cold cream. As she smoothed it on and then removed it gently with a tissue, she thought of her mother.

She had watched her do this since childhood and remembered her saying how important it was to clean her face nightly. The ritual brought back good memories and somehow lessened her feelings of loss.

She carried a glass of water, put it on her nightstand, and got under the covers. Rescue crept under and snuggled next to her knees. They went to sleep with the light still on.

CHAPTER

9

After she showered and washed her hair, she put on a crisp white shirt and dark skirt. She pulled her hair into a low ponytail that curled around her neck. Then she applied mascara and lipstick. She had never been vain about her appearance and disliked spending time trying to improve the way she looked, instead of doing what she considered to be more important things on her To Do list. Luckily, she had a naturally pleasing appearance without any fuss. However, she was going to visit Macon County Social Services, where her mother had worked, for the first time since her mother died, and she wanted to look professional. She wanted to show respect for the professional workers there. Many of the social workers remembered her as a young girl so she also wanted to be taken seriously as a reporter.

Ready to go, she set out fresh water and food for Rescue

and went to her father's house across the driveway.

Lucas and Ed were having breakfast at the table.

"Do you want to join us?" Lucas asked.

"No thanks, but I do have more questions about the Swan family."

Lucas set his fork down and shook his head. "I told you enough. They're bad news. Keep away from them. They've been criminals longer than I've been a lawyer, and you know how long that is."

"I'm not going anywhere until you help me with this." Daisy took a seat directly opposite Lucas. "I'm not planning on going to see if Keira is with her family. I don't think she is."

Lucas nodded. "Glad to hear that."

"I'm just worried because of all the secrecy. Keira's just vanished into thin air again. She left her baby with Lexie, not with her folks. If I knew why, I might be able to find her, to help her.

"Listen: Keira's like a wraith that blew in with the fog and faded away as the sun rose." Daisy did not know what else to say to convince her father. "I'm very worried about her."

Lucas rose from the table.

"Let's go talk on the porch."

As Ed cleared the table and began to wash the dishes, Daisy and her father went out. They sat in the old rocking chairs. Daisy waited for Lucas to begin the conversation.

"Do you remember Keira's grandfather? George Swan. George Arthur Swan, to be exact."

"Didn't he come to our church?"

"Later in life." Lucas snorted. "I guess he worried about

if he'd get to heaven or not."

Daisy remembered him as a sallow-skinned old man in an old-fashioned suit, double-breasted with wide lapels. She nodded and Lucas continued, "He was quite ill then. Lung cancer after years of smoking. He passed away the month before Keira was born.

"He was born mean and didn't improve with age. Mean as a copperhead with its fangs in a rabbit. If he thought he could get away with something, he'd do it and wouldn't look back. And he was always that way."

"Did you know him a long time?"

"We were in school at the same time. He was a little older as I recall and was a typical playground bully. Stealing money. Stealing books when he'd lost his. It wasn't that he was bigger than everybody. He wasn't. Like I said he was just plain mean, a mean scrapper.

"He skipped school as often as he could get away with it. When he was old enough, he dropped out and began stealing and smuggling drugs, alcohol, and cigarettes."

"Why would he smuggle alcohol and cigarettes? They're legal here."

"Two reasons, "Lucas answered. "To avoid taxes and to sell to minors. If anybody came snooping around or interfered with his activities, they'd disappear. Eventually law enforcement gave up and ignored him as long as he stayed out of the *good* parts of town."

"That's awful!" Daisy could not imagine Sheriff Ben Williams taking that attitude. "How do the Swans manage to skirt the law nowadays?"

"They try to keep a low profile. They grow marijuana. Do small deals for cash. They worked for Walker to sell his drugs in Franklin. They shoplift for food, clothing…for anything they need that they can find in stores," Lucas said. "In fact, I think they were pretty relieved when George passed. Keira's father was in and out of jail, and his brother Bud (George, Jr.) served a stretch in prison for transporting across state lines. They quit running things up from Atlanta when he got caught. That left room for Walker to move in."

"Poor Keira," Daisy said. "No wonder she ran away back then, but I still don't understand why she's left Brad and Lexie's now."

When Ed joined them on the porch, Daisy got up to leave. "Nothing personal Ed. I've got to get to work. See y'all tonight."

The Macon County Department of Social Services would be open, but Daisy did not want to tell Lucas where she was going for fear of bringing up sad memories. Six years ago, her mother's work took her to a forgotten mountain road where she died in a single-car crash. Daisy and her father still grieved. She refused to believe the crash was an accident and was going to speak with her mother's former colleagues to learn more about the call that drew her to that place.

Daisy turned off Lakeside Drive into the parking lot for a complex of buildings that housed several county services. She took a visitor space and entered the Department of Social Services. Having been to her mother's office many times in the past, she walked directly there.

She did not know the young woman at the reception desk and stopped to introduce herself.

"We haven't met," Daisy said. I'm Daisy McLaren. My

mother used to work here. Can you tell Patricia Sanford that I'm here and would like to see her, if she's free?"

The receptionist was on the phone a minute and then said, "She'll be right here."

Daisy sat down and thumbed through an old copy of *Our State* that featured towns in the North Carolina mountains. She had barely begun an article on the Smoky Mountain Center for the Performing Arts in Franklin when Patricia came stomping into the waiting room.

"Daisy dear!" Patricia said. "Let me take a look at you." She took Daisy by the shoulders and looked her over. "I can't believe we don't run into each other around this small town. Different schedules, I guess. Come on back. Gloria will be so surprised to see you."

Patricia and Gloria Hill had worked alongside Alice McLaren for years and had observed Daisy as she grew up. Her mother began working there when Daisy entered Franklin Elementary School. Patricia was already one of the county's social workers, and Gloria came on board several years later. They each had private offices where they met with clients, but Patricia led Daisy to a larger conference room where Gloria waited.

"You're a sight for sore eyes!" Gloria said. "Let me look at you child." She rushed over and hugged Daisy.

Patricia interrupted. "Let's sit over here." She indicated chairs at the long table and took the one at the head. "Did you miss us?'

Daisy sat down and said, "Well, yes, but that's not really why I'm here."

"Of course, I see." Patricia looked down and twisted her wedding ring. "Do you still have questions?"

Daisy had not taken time to sort out her feelings from questions for which she needed answers. Confusion furrowed her brow as she looked from one to the other. She had been sure of the reasons for her visit as she had driven over. She wanted details of the last time they had seen Alice. Conversations they had in her last days. Now that she was there, one question was dominant.

Do you think my mother was murdered?

CHAPTER

10

Why would we think that?" Patricia was the first to speak. "Sheriff Williams investigated it thoroughly and concluded that it was an accident. He couldn't find any signs of another car or any people in the area. Surely it was an accident."

Gloria reached out, took Daisy's hand, and held it between her own hands. "Honey child, it must be torture to even think that." She gently patted Daisy's hand. "You must rest your mind about that. Nobody didn't like Alice as far as I know. She'd helped many people, well-off and poor, in Franklin. Folk respected her and your father. Now rest easy. Let me get you some water."

Gloria left the room. Patricia also stood while Daisy remained seated, looking up at her and asking, "Don't you find it odd that she was even on that road? There's nothing out there."

Before she could answer, Gloria came back and handed Daisy the water.

"Now drink that up and rest a bit," she said. "Trish is right. If there was any bad stuff going on, the sheriff would have found it."

Daisy remembered that in Gloria's book, Sheriff Williams could do no wrong ever since he did not arrest her son Keshawn the first time that he caught him with marijuana. He had taken him home and arranged with Gloria and her husband for Keshawn to do some work around his office. He had figured rightly that, seeing the sorts of people he put in jail, Keshawn would be less likely to do illegal things. Today Keshawn Hill was a Macon County Deputy Sheriff.

"Thank you," Daisy said. Gloria comforted her with caring, perhaps because she knew how it felt to be always struggling. A Pell Grant got Gloria through college. Fellowships allowed her to gain a Master of Arts in social work, but that came with hours of teaching and reading the papers of undergraduates.

Still sitting at the head of the table, Patricia brusquely said, "If that's all, we need to get back to work."

Gloria ignored her. "Did you have anything else you wanted to know?"

Daisy silently thanked her with her eyes. "Yes, there is. You worked with my mother for many years and knew her better than anyone."

She sipped the water and set it on the table cupped between her hands.

"I'm trying to understand why she would go alone to such a deserted area, and I thought that you might help.

Maybe something happened in her final days at work that could shed some light."

Patricia spoke first again. "At work Alice was perfectly normal. A dedicated worker. As Gloria said, well-liked. My understanding was that she got a phone call that caused her to drive out there."

"But Trish, that's not entirely true."

Gloria gently shook her head and turned to Daisy.

"For a couple of weeks before she died, Alice had kept to herself here. She was pleasant enough, but didn't really talk to me, or anyone else, as she usually did.

"More and more she was out of the office without putting on the board where she would be," she said referring to the whiteboard where the staff was supposed to write the time they left, destination, client's name, and time they expected to return. "Then again, she rarely even came in."

Patricia interrupted. "We all do that sometimes when..."

"But not every day and that last week it was every day for Alice."

Gloria paused as though she was not sure about saying, "Then there was the matter of the missing files."

"That was nothing," Patricia muttered.

"At least 25 to 30 of Alice's case files disappeared," Gloria continued. "She had not signed them out as we're supposed to, but we assumed she took them."

"I've got to get back to work."

Patricia stood and waited a moment for Gloria to join her before leaving the room. Gloria remained. Patricia left them alone.

Daisy shuddered, fearing she already knew the answer, and asked, "What kind of cases were they?"

Gloria cast her glance down as she recalled, "Young girls from all around the area were reported missing. She was obsessed with them and was determined to find out where they were, what had happened to them.

"You're so much like your mother, child. I reckon you're not going to give up this bone until you find the answer. Just please be careful. If her death had anything to do with those cases, it could still be dangerous to go snooping around."

Tired of people constantly cautioning her to avoid potentially dangerous situations, Daisy took the easy way and did not argue.

"I will." However, she was already considering what to do next when Gloria added, "It was at the same time Alice died that we discovered the files were missing. Only files relating to the missing women."

"Did you ever find them?"

"No, we didn't. Lucas even let us search their home. Still nothing." Gloria shook her head and exhaled a deep sigh of regret. "Patricia decided that someone had destroyed them for an unknown reason, but that didn't make sense to anyone else."

"Thanks for being honest with me. Patricia acted so strange, like she didn't want to be bothered by me. Do you think she was jealous of Mom, or what?"

"Dear child, I don't rightly know. She'd always tried to oversee the department. Made decisions without consulting me or any of the other social workers. It was easier for her to do that after Alice died." She hesitated before asking, "Do you really think she was murdered?"

Was her mother really murdered? The question lingered in Daisy's mind as she drove back into town. Shaken by the implication that her mother had stolen files from her department, she felt that once again her father had withheld information from her. Information that could shed light on her mother's death, which now Daisy was convinced was, yes, murder. *Why didn't Dad tell me this? What could have happened to those files? Did Patricia destroy them?*

Daisy had never really cared for Patricia, nor had her mother. Her appearance matched her personality. Severe and dry. Gaunt. Unyielding. Dyed hair. Bangs cut in an unsuccessful attempt to cover her wrinkled brow and to appear younger than she was. All-in-all, like someone who did not enjoy life or the many pleasures it offered.

Was there a file on Keira?

In her distress she had forgotten all about Keira. She should have asked if Keira had a social worker assigned to help her when she became pregnant. They might know where she had been since last November. Or had Keira been forgotten, brushed to the side, as her mother had been. Patricia seemed eager for Daisy to leave without gaining any knowledge about the files. If she needed more help from DSS, she would contact Gloria directly.

If her mother had actually taken them, where could they be? She would have taken them for a reason, perhaps to safeguard them. Her mother was intent on finding out what happened to the young women and would have protected the files that might contain clues. But what if they had been in the car when she died? If she were murdered, as Daisy suspected, her killer might have carried them off. Perhaps she was killed because she had the files.

CHAPTER

11

Daisy pulled into the parking lot behind Lucas's law office and entered through the back door. His door was closed so she continued until she reached Maxie's office.

Maxie was titled as the office administrator, and she held the reins in a tight grip. No one could barge into the office to see Lucas without an appointment. If they managed to convince Maxie that they had a legitimate reason to see him, they had to endure a long wait before being escorted to his office.

Lucas had encouraged her to become certified as a paralegal and paid for her to spend a semester in Chapel Hill to attend the program at the university. After completion she breezed through the qualifying examination and began to assist him by preparing drafts of documents in civil cases. Once Lucas reviewed the drafts, she typed the final documents for signatures and filing.

Daisy learned a lot about the law when she worked with Maxie one summer. She learned enough to realize it was not the exciting career the public visualized. No Jake Brigance or Theodore Boones here. Just a lot of typing legal descriptions of real estate with the occasional DUI thrown in.

No matter how busy she was, she always made time for Franklin teenagers with broken hearts or hangovers, and she always had time for Daisy. She was the only person who could console Daisy after her mother's death. She continued to act as both a friend and mother figure for her through the years, and when Maxie's husband died, it was to Daisy she turned for support. Like Ed, Maxie was family, and this family was a small but close group of people who loved each other.

Maybe Maxie could tell her where to find the files.

She was on the phone when Daisy entered her office. She quickly got rid of the caller and held out her left hand to reveal a ruby and diamond ring.

"Seriously?" Daisy asked.

"David made it official last night." Maxie was beaming, resplendent in a black wrap-around dress that set off her pendant with the large ruby her father had found and had made into a pendant for her mother. Her engagement ring completed the stunning picture.

"When? Where?" Daisy was sputtering from excitement. "Can I be your maid of honor?"

Laughing at Daisy's enthusiasm, she replied, "You can be a witness. We're keeping it simple. We've got the license and we're having the ceremony at the church, probably at the end of July."

She had dated David Tenant, the pharmacist at the Franklin Walmart since last fall, but they had known each other for years before that in an adult Sunday School class at First United Methodist. When her husband died, that class had been a support community, and her connection with all the people in it grew. When she accepted David's invitation to go out for dinner, she accepted as a friend. She surprised herself when she developed stronger feelings for him. By the time he asked her to marry him, there was no doubt about her response.

Daisy was shocked at first. She knew how broken-hearted Maxie had been when she lost her husband. As she thought about it, it made sense. A person's feelings for another could change over time.

"That's wonderful! I'm so happy for you, and David."

Then she changed topics.

"What's Dad doing? I need to talk to him as soon as I can."

"I don't know. He closed his door and made a call around 20 minutes ago. You want me to call you when he's free?"

"I'll wait. I'll just go sit up front. Did Dad tell you about Keira and the baby?"

"He did. I just can't see her going off like that for no reason. She worked hard to make something of herself. I'm fairly sure she and Joe Taylor had a thing. She must've had a rough time when he overdosed. No, I think the only reason she left that baby was to protect it."

Daisy sat and took out the small black notebook she always carried for notetaking. She pulled aside the elastic strap which held it closed and turned to the page marked with a ribbon, where she made notes about Keira.

Who was the father of her baby?

Why had she left it with Lexie instead of with her family?

Did she leave on her own, or did someone take her?

Who picked her up on Wayah Road?

Where is she now?!?!?

She thumbed open to another page to add questions about her mother.

Why had her mother been working away from the office?

Had she taken the missing files? Where are they now?

Who had called and given her the tip that caused her to go to the road where she died?

Had she been murdered?

Was her murderer someone in Franklin? Someone they all knew?

The final question sent a shudder up her spine. She had grown up in Franklin and, through her work as a reporter, had come to know most people outside of her circle of friends and family. She could not imagine anyone she knew being involved in any of these events.

Looking outside of that group, she figured that the Swans would be high on a list of suspects. Last fall a drug smuggler known only as Christian hinted that he had known her mother but died before he could tell her how. Jasmine Walker had shot and killed him.

Lucas left his office and came down the hall using a walker.

"Daddy! Are you okay?"

Daisy rushed over to help him.

"Stop fussing. Please. The doctor just recommended

that I use this, so I don't overtax my legs. Only use it in the office. Go on back and I'll join you in a minute."

Lucas stepped into Maxie's office.

"Please get me an appointment with the D.A. I'll need about 30 minutes with him. Tell him we need to discuss Lem Hawkins."

Daisy remembered the incident the previous fall when he was arrested for a DUI. He had fallen asleep in his truck on the side of the road. Lucas had worked it out so Lem could drive to and from his work in construction as well as for essential work activities.

When Lucas rejoined his daughter, she asked, "What's happened with Lem?'

Lucas paused but, knowing that Daisy would not gossip, said, "Off the record, he was stopped driving downtown last night and he had been drinking. You remember he's still on probation with restricted driving."

"Oh no, poor Sandra."

Sandra had been in Daisy's class at Franklin High, and they had often studied together. While Daisy was able to go away for college, Sandra stayed in Franklin and worked in downtown stores until she became pregnant and married Lem.

"I'm hoping to get him into a good rehab program instead of jail."

Daisy thought how Sandra would need a lot of support, emotional and financial, and she began to figure out what she could do to help.

"What can I do for you?"

The question drew Daisy back to her present mission, finding Keira.

"Keira is still missing. I went by Mom's old office and Gloria told me that the files on the girls had disappeared. She and Patricia thought one possibility was that Mom had taken them. I hope that, if I can find them, they might contain clues about what has happened to Keira."

She paused and drew a breath before asking, "Do you know where they are?"

Lucas shook his head. "No, and I searched for them when I learned they were lost. They weren't in the car. If Ali had them, I can't imagine where she kept them."

"She wouldn't have destroyed them. If she took them, she would've had a good reason." Daisy sat and put her head in her hands. "And Keira wouldn't have left her baby without a good reason. I just have to find her."

CHAPTER

12

Main Street was lively with a swarm of tourists returning from a busy morning of gem hunting to eat lunch and shop for souvenirs, or perhaps for gems they had failed to find at the mines. Identifying them as gem hunters was easy. Sunburnt. Eager. Holding plastic shopping bags plump with souvenir purchases. Locals avoided Main Street in the afternoon unless they had specific business to conduct. It was crowded and the free parking spaces were practically nonexistent.

Daisy's cell chimed. Jake, probably asking if she wants to get lunch together. She let it go to voicemail. Jake was overprotective, in Daisy's opinion. He had been ever since she returned to Franklin after her mother's death. Daisy knew he wanted to resume the relationship they had had in high school, when he had been not only her best friend but also her boyfriend.

She had an experience in Chapel Hill that left her resistant to his attempts, until the previous fall when she nursed him back to health. Caring for him drew her closer, but in her heart she knew she would have to tell him what happened in Chapel Hill. There should be no wall between them.

And before she could tell Jake, she would have to tell Lucas and Ed. She did not know which would be harder.

Fearful of what could happen to Daisy, Jake had warned her over and over not to go off on her own while investigating the plane crash on the mountain where the Walker and Simpson families lived, and Daisy chose to ignore his warnings. In the end, her bullheadedness caused Jake to be wounded.

As she helped care for him as he healed, they grew closer. During the following winter and into the spring the bond between them strengthened, but Daisy still kept him at arm's length. He could not break down the barrier between them. She thought about returning Jake's call, but she had already reached the bookstore and decided that call could wait.

Two displays stood in pride of place in the bookstore. A rack holding Charles Frazier's book stood by a new one for a new local author who had written a book about the crimes and murders of the previous fall titled *Murder on the Mountain*.

In the center of the store Jasmine Walker, elbows on the counter, held Brad's attention. Observing them for a moment, Daisy wondered what they could discuss so seriously that they did not notice her. Brad, scowling, leaning across the counter so he was right in Jasmine's face, was clearly arguing. Jasmine was not moving back, not backing down. Instead, she shoved Brad's shoulders. As he tried to hold his own, he twisted around and saw Daisy, frozen at the front of the store. Attempting to appear normal, Daisy moved slowly to join the two.

"I hope I'm not interrupting," she said as she reached the sales counter.

"Of course not," Jasmine said brusquely. "I was just leaving. Later, Brad."

Brad nodded as she exited.

"How are you doing, Daisy? Strange about Keira, isn't it?"

He placed a small carton of books on the counter.

"Can I help you with anything?"

"What was that about?'

"Another satisfied customer!"

Brad tried to pass it off as a joke, but Daisy refused to let it go by.

"Brad, Jasmine pushed you, pretty hard, and you looked like you wanted to bite her head off."

The normally placid Brad snapped back, "You need to learn when to back off. This is none of your business."

He shook his head.

"Sorry Daisy. You know how Jasmine thinks the world should revolve around her. I just felt that I had to get her off her high horse. Needless to say, it did not go over very well with her."

Daisy was still shocked by the scene she had witnessed but decided to drop it. Returning to her primary mission, she said, "Actually, I hope you can tell me where the Swans live. It doesn't seem likely that she would go to them, but I think it's worth a look."

Brad relaxed and replied, "You know they are tough customers? All I know is that they have always lived in a mobile home park south on the Atlanta Highway. No idea which lot they'd be on."

"That's enough to get me started. Is Lexie here?"

"Nope. At home with Alexa."

He returned to his work as Daisy left the store.

Main Street was still bustling. As cars were backed out of spaces, others immediately took the spots. Jasmine was fixing to get in a red and white Mini Cooper. Daisy called out as she rushed over, "Jasmine, wait up."

Jasmine scowled but paused with the door open to let Daisy reach her.

"What was that with Brad?"

"He didn't have a book I ordered weeks ago. No big deal."

"You looked awfully angry to be just upset about a book, and Brad was furious. What's the book?"

"Just a book. From the best sellers' list. I can't think of the name."

Daisy touched Jasmine's arm and studied her to see if she was telling the truth. There was more to know, but clearly neither would give in.

"Never mind," she said and moved back to the sidewalk. She could smell rain in the air and rushed to her car to check out the trailer park where the Swans lived. She hoped to get there before the storm arrived.

As she started to back out, Jasmine sped past in her sporty car. She had long admired Jasmine, and Jasmine had probably saved her life last fall, but then again, she did have that *entitled* attitude Brad had described.

Maybe I'll call to get together for lunch one day. After all, I never really thanked her for rescuing me at the ruby mine.

CHAPTER

13

As Daisy drove toward the Georgia Highway, burgeoning clouds stormed across the western sky. Remembering the downpour that took control of her Jeep last fall and hoping to avoid being trapped in another deluge on another mountain, she floored the accelerator.

Her business at the mobile home park should not take long. She would locate the Swan home and perhaps knock on the door to ask for Keira. Then either go home or back to Lucas's law office. No harm in that.

Daisy had always felt immune to jeopardy, in spite of events in her past. She felt that her core, her center, remained protected just as she had been protected by her family before her mother died. Instead of unsettling Daisy's faith in the permanence of family, that loss tightened the bond between her and her father, and she had chosen to remain in Franklin where she had always felt safe.

When the road crossed the Appalachian Highway, orange cones marking lane closures for construction and cars slowing so the drivers could decide which fast food restaurant looked good for dinner frustrated Daisy. She was forced to creep along. She passed the new Ingles Supermarket and was able to speed up. She passed other stores and businesses, including the Ruby Theater, where the town came together every weekend.

Finally, she was well past the business district, so she slowed the red Compass Sport and scanned both sides of the road for signs of a community where the Swans might be found. Approaching the small Otto community, she noticed a rusted metal sign announcing Hillside Mobile Home Park. She had already passed the entrance to the park, so she turned into the Old School Knife Works parking lot to turn back.

Fearing she might miss the entrance again, she drove at the speed limit, slowed, and turned on her right turn signal when she thought she was close. Still, it surprised her. There it was. She took a sharp turn and steered the Jeep up the road until she came in sight of the park where home after home plastered the hill. She had not expected so many mobile homes and was uncertain of how to proceed. At least the road was asphalt with few potholes which she could easily dodge.

Downshifting to second gear, she crept along, looking around for signs that might show that a family like the Swans might live there. She peered down the crossroads and, down one, saw a young woman walking a dog, a spaniel. She turned into the road, parked, and climbed out.

Upon spying her, the brown and white dog strained against her leash and dragged her hapless owner toward Daisy. Reaching her, she sprang up to place her paws on Daisy's chest. The nub of a tail wagged furiously with joy.

"Down, Poppy!" the owner commanded. Poppy ignored the order and tried to lick Daisy's face. Daisy took the dog's paws, set them firmly on the ground, and said, "Sit!" Poppy sat.

"Good girl."

The young woman approached them.

"How'd you do that? She never listens to me."

Daisy, considering how to respond and deciding that honesty was indeed the best policy here, said, "She doesn't think you mean it. You could probably use some training."

Daisy hoped she had not offended the woman and relaxed when she chuckled.

"You're so right! Poppy is such a good girl, but so stubborn. You aren't by any chance a trainer, are you?"

"Sorry. I'm Daisy McLaren, a reporter. I know Poppy." Daisy laughed. "What's your name?"

"Angela Wolfe. And you're so right about who needs to be trained."

"I'm looking for the Swans' home. Do you know them?"

"I don't actually know them, but I know where they live. You go to the top where the road dead-ends at the woods. They're in the second lot. In fact, they have two lots. You can't miss 'em."

Daisy thanked her and backed onto the road going uphill. Entering the road at the top of the community, she saw that she could have picked out where the Swans lived without asking. Two mobile homes connected by a ramshackle walkway. Cinder blocks formed steps at the center of this boardwalk. There were no safety rails either by the stairs or along the walkway.

She had been so focused on locating the Swans that she had not noticed the darkening sky which threatened rain at any moment. Now she did, and common sense told her she should drive home at once. But her need to find Keira overruled common sense.

What's the harm in simply knocking on the door and asking for Keira? None.

CHAPTER

14

Daisy pulled over to the edge of the road and got out. As she did, a few heavy drops of rain plopped on the ground and on her head. "Dang," she said aloud but kept moving toward the cinder block steps. Which trailer? She opted for the one on the left and hurried toward it.

Up close it looked worse than it had from the road, and that was bad. The storm door had been removed from the home and was on the ground below. The vinyl siding had been neglected, probably since the mobile home had first been set in place. Where it had not been tinted green from rampant algae growth, it was black with mildew. The door that remained was dirty where hands had pushed it open, and it bore the scuff marks near the bottom edge where it had been kicked many times. Who knows why? Pockmarks in the siding. From gunshots? Daisy tried not to speculate.

She pressed the doorbell button but did not hear it ring. When no one came to the door, she rapped on it several times. Still, no one responded.

Gusts of wind pushed against her, and a driving rain soon followed. The only shelter available other than the trailer was her car, and she still had no idea of Keira's whereabouts. Hesitating for only a moment, Daisy turned the knob and cautiously entered the home. "Hello," she called out. "Anyone home? It's Daisy McLaren."

No answer.

CHAPTER

15

She closed the door behind her, then she felt the wall until she found the light switch and flipped it up. Nothing happened. She was still in darkness and saw only shapeless dark shadows. The storm must have downed the power lines. She waited until her eyes adjusted enough to sharpen the edges of these dark forms. Moving quickly again, she banged her shin into a low coffee table. "Ouch!" She slowed down.

Treading softly among the clutter with her arms outstretched and feeling side to side for other hazards, she felt like Frankenstein (or was that his monster?). She had to remind herself that, despite feelings of guilt over the fact she was breaking and entering, she was the good guy here. Seeking Keira who could be held captive in one of these homes.

Daisy wished she had not forgotten to bring her phone

in her rush to get inside before the unexpected storm hit. The iPhone flashlight would have come in handy. But for the heavy rain pummeling the roof of the trailer and the road, she would have dashed out to retrieve it. Instead, she continued along, seeking a solid wall to guide her.

At last, she found it. A long hall stretched before her with windows on the outer wall and rooms to the left. She pulled up each window shade, but only scant light penetrated the darkness. Upon reaching the first door, she rapped lightly and whispered, "Hello?" She tapped on the hollow wood door again, and when there was no answer, she turned the doorknob and pushed it open.

A crack and a flash of thunder and lightning startled Daisy, and she drew back from the opened door. Hearing a noise behind her, she turned and thought she saw a brief light. She froze and waited. When nothing happened, she convinced herself that it was her imagination. Nothing else. Probably more lightning, distant or lighting up the clouds.

Inching along, she peeked into a second room where the door had been left open. A bathroom.

She waited a bit longer and then moved on to the third door. She knocked softly but immediately opened the door without waiting for a reply. She stepped in and quickly realized that they used the room for storage. She felt around and could tell that it was jam-packed with stuff—cardboard boxes, plastic garbage bags probably filled with clothes.

This room was as dark and dank as the previous one. Such a musty smell did not happen overnight. For a moment she was glad the electricity was off and that she could not turn on lights as she imagined mold, mildew, spiders, mice, and rats. When she heard the scratchy sounds of small creatures skittering in the darkness, she backed into the hall and shut the door.

The place was creeping her out, but as she moved through without encountering anyone, her confidence grew. One door remained. She strode to the third door facing her at the end of the hall and knocked confidently and shouted, "Hello! Anyone there?" She tried to turn the door but could not. Why would this door be locked when the others were not?

She banged with her fist on the door and shouted but got no response. On TV she had seen private detectives and impatient cops open locked doors using a credit card, but she had left her bag with wallet and credit cards in the car.

As she turned to go out, a fist seemed to come from nowhere and everything turned black.

CHAPTER

16

Daisy woke up slowly and found herself in a car. A thick mist coated the exterior of the windows and windshield. She touched the left side of her face, felt a lump, and drew her hand back. Her head was throbbing. She groaned and lay back. As she became more aware, she knew she was stretched out on the back seat of a car. Not just any car, but her own Jeep.

She sat up and, after wiping the windows, was able to see a dense gray fog enveloping the trees beside the road on one side. She cleared the window on the other side where the fog partially concealed an overgrown clearing. Low bushes grew close, mountain laurels, and beyond, a small tin-roofed cabin sat in the middle. Her foggy brain had the idea that whoever lived there could help her. She shivered, not from cold as it was a steamy day in July, rather from the uncertainty of her situation.

Daisy leaned forward to look in the front seat. Her bag was there, and inside it was her phone. The battery still had power, but of course there was no reception. That would have made things too easy for her. Her chest grew tight, and her breathing was rapid, heralding a panic attack on the horizon. *Slow down. Breathe slowly and deeply.* She commanded her body to relax and began the deep breathing that would calm her. Her therapy sessions with Dr. Ammons were paying off. *Note to self: contact Dr. Ammons for an appointment.*

The cabin was quiet. Its curtains were drawn, and shades were down. No smoke rose from the stone chimney. Taking her cell phone, Daisy stepped out of the Jeep onto an old road which had lost most of its gravel and now had channels, large and small, which rivulets of water had etched into the packed earth over time. She walked carefully through the weedy yard. Aware that snakes could be slithering in the overgrown brush, she took a step, stopped, and proceeded when nothing rattled at her or struck out. She continued to breathe deeply.

Weathered and splintery wooden steps led to the door. She stepped over the bottom one which was clearly rotting away. The brown door had also been battered over time by storms, and the cheap veneer had rippled and cracked at the lowest edge. She needed to pee but decided that she could wait for the bathroom she assumed would be in the cabin. She stopped and leaned her head against the door to listen for any sounds of life but heard nothing.

"Daisy, stop it," she imagined Jake saying. "Get in and get back to town." That thought sparked her headstrong determination to find out what was inside. Never one to be put off a trail, she was unshakeable when challenged, and since she believed this place would hold clues to the identity of the person who had slugged her, she was more determined than ever. Remembering the previous attack, she checked her phone again. Still no reception, so she pressed the icon for flashlight.

Without knocking, Daisy tried the front door. Unlocked. She pushed it open.

She panned the room with the cell's flashlight, and then she tried the light switch beside the door, but nothing happened. Whether there was no power because of the storm or because no one had paid the electric bill little mattered to her. The flashlight on her cell gave her the confidence to move forward.

Either shades or curtains covered the windows, so she started with those to her left and lifted the roller shades up to look out on the front yard. Then she drew back the curtains on a window. She crossed the room that stretched across the front of the house and drew open the curtains there.

Additional light through the windows let her see the room, but she kept the flashlight on as she studied the space. The kitchen was clean and tidy. A dish drainer on a blue rubber mat held clean glasses. Opening several cupboards, she found them mostly empty, a few mismatched plates, mugs, an empty Nabisco Saltines tin, and some ant traps.

The refrigerator held only a 24-pack of Dasani. There was no table. No chairs. A large blue sectional and matching loveseat, covered with a cheap imitation velvet fabric, were the only other furnishings.

Now urgently needing a toilet, she shone the iPhone

light down the hall. Trying the first door on the left, she sighed with relief. A bathroom. She set her phone on the edge of the sink, so it still lit up the room. When finished, she pulled up her jeans, washed her hands, and continued down the hall. A mirror over the sink reflected her face with a lump just above her eye which merged with her swollen eyelids. Hoping to find Tylenol, she opened the medicine cabinet. Empty. She took her iPhone and returned to the hall.

The next door was locked, as were the other two across the hall. Frustrated, she thought about getting a credit card from the car, but quickly realized the doors were locked with deadbolts that required a key to open from the hall. She called out Keira's name but got no reply.

Back in the kitchen, she got a bottle of water. She drank it quickly and grabbed another to take to the car. She had no idea where she was or how long it would take her to get home. She went outside and stood for a moment on the stoop. To the left she saw an old smokehouse. Better left for another day.

Daisy walked carefully back to her Jeep. Before turning the key, she pulled down the visor to check out her face. Besides the lump, now her left eye had swollen and was tinted purple and red. Her headache was worsening.

She drove until she reached a paved road. She stopped to call Jake. Certainly, he would yell at her and berate her for going out alone, but then he would hold her tight. She would feel safe in his arms.

CHAPTER

17

The Appalachian Mountains surrounding the long valley where Franklin lay contain some of the oldest rocks on Earth. When the Iapetus Ocean flooded North America during the Paleozoic Era, the ridges and sediment valleys took shape with layers of alternating hard and soft sedimentary rock. As erosion began to shape the landscape, the hard layers of sandstone or chert resisted, while the soft areas of shale or limestone eroded more easily. This process slowly developed into the ridges and valleys of today and greatly influenced the soil composition of the two. The process is ongoing but is exceedingly slow. Such large valleys and ridges have been created because it started 200 million years ago.

The types of sedimentary rocks also greatly influenced the types of soils they produced as erosion took effect. On the ridges, slightly acidic soils supported tree growth while the valleys collected more fertile soils that would one day attract farmers, such as Jake's ancestors, to the region. Daisy had learned about all of this in geology class, popular at Franklin High because of the mountains.

The rising sun and summer's heat burned off the fog as Daisy drove on, but she was still in the shadow of an eastern ridge. Ahead she saw daylight slowly traveling down another mountain ridge. The sun was lighting up trees, rivers, and rocks, creating shadows moving across the valleys and up the western ridges. By noon, the sun would be high and would banish the shadows. As the sun passed over the meridian and afternoon began, the process reversed until the sun would set and all would be dark.

At last, she crossed a bridge over the river she recognized as the Cullasaja. She now had her bearings so, when she came to a road where traffic whizzed by, she recognized it as the road between Franklin and Highlands and turned toward home. The ancient Cullasaja Gorge, created by eons of water and wind erosion, roared behind her.

She thought of calling her father but figured that Jake had already notified him that she was all right, and Jake, once his relief at hearing her voice had passed, had given her a loud and harsh lecture which would suffice for the both of them. Her head was throbbing wildly, and she considered stopping at the first store she came to for Extra-Strength Excedrin. As a part of his tirade, Jake had admonished her plainly to drive straight to the Emergency Room at the Mission Hospital and that he would meet her there. As she felt her face with its goose-egg lump and swollen eyelid, she decided to take his advice for once.

Feeling that the drive was taking forever, Daisy was surprised when the directional signs pointed out the way to the Mission Hospital Emergency Room. She stopped the Jeep in front of the automatic doors and climbed out. Jake rushed out and embraced her. Daisy hid her face against his chest and sobbed in relief.

"There. There," Jake said. "Go ahead and cry. You've been through the wringer. I…we're just glad you came out in one piece. I told Lucas not to come and that I'd bring you to his house when you're taken care of here if that's what you want."

Daisy sniffed and nodded. "Thanks. I don't want him to worry. How long was I gone?"

"Since noon yesterday. Since you hadn't told anyone where you were going, Lucas started worrying when you didn't call or show up for dinner.

"Later that evening Ed went to get Rescue."

Daisy began to cry again at the thought of the little calico waiting for her to come home and feed her.

"Everybody's okay now. Thankful that you are safe with us."

"Keira?"

"Still no word."

"The baby?"

"Alexa is with my mom. She's gonna be spoiled rotten by the time Keira gets back."

A nurse came to take them from the triage area to a private examination room, and Jake went to park Daisy's car.

By the time he got back, the nurse was talking with Daisy. She had helped her change from the clothes now gathered in a plastic bag, into a gown and she had given Daisy an ice pack to hold against her eye. She was using a form on her iPad to take history and allergic reactions. She finally asked why she was there today, as if it were not obvious.

Jake took over and explained to the nurse that Daisy had been missing since yesterday and that she had awakened in an isolated cabin with the injuries. The last thing she remembered was turning and being hit. As she questioned Daisy, the nurse took her temperature and blood pressure. Once finished, she left them alone.

Daisy and Jake sat and waited. He took the opportunity to embrace her tenderly as he helped her move from the chair where she had been left to the examining table. He helped her stretch out with a pillow under her head. Then he planted a kiss on her forehead.

"You gotta quit scaring me like that! Not to mention Lucas and Ed. Even the cats were antsy all night."

Jake was rubbing her hand gently as he spoke, and his voice was also gentle. Daisy tried to think of a wisecrack to throw at him but could think of nothing.

"Thanks for coming."

She spoke softly and turned away to block the tears she felt rising again.

"Dad?"

Jake did not point out that he had already told her about Lucas and answered, "He's waiting at the house. I told him I'd bring you home when we're finished here."

They heard a familiar voice in the hall. A light rap on the door. Sheriff Ben Williams entered the room. Daisy and Jake knew him from the time he was their history teacher at

Franklin High School. Not long after they graduated, he ran for sheriff, won by a landslide, and has won every election since. Daisy prepared for what she presumed would be a lecture.

"Daisy McLaren. How are you feeling? Not too well, I reckon."

CHAPTER

18

Before Daisy could answer, the doctor entered the room with the same nurse. She thought she knew everyone in town. But not this doctor. Black longish hair, sparkling blue eyes, and a beard, full but neatly trimmed. He resembled more the backpackers who passed through town on their way to hike the Appalachian Trail than a doctor. *I could write a feature story about him.* He interrupted her thoughts with, "Hello Miss McLaren, I'm Dr. Thibaut."

He indicated the door for Jake and Ben to step out while he examined her. Ben took the plastic bag of clothes.

The doctor then turned his gaze on her.

"Daisy."

"What?"

"Call me Daisy. Everyone does."

Tall, dark, and handsome, he studied the iPad for a

minute and then returned to her. Her outer clothing had been handed over to Ben to hold in case they needed DNA evidence. Now she wore a little blue and white print hospital gown tied in the back. She reached around to make sure the back was as securely closed as it could be.

Dr. Thibaut took out a small light and shone it briefly in each of her eyes. "Follow my finger with your eyes. Don't move your head. Just your eyes." He next looked in each ear, listened to her heart, and checked her breathing.

"You seem to be okay, except for the obvious."

Daisy managed a small laugh.

"Your head took a severe blow. There's a chance of a concussion. I'm ordering a CT scan now. We can do that here. That will let us know if you have any bleeding in the brain." He paused. "You might need an MRI as well, but we'll do that another day, if necessary.

"I'm giving you a prescription for Percocet. Just a few because it contains oxycodone and acetaminophen. If you still have a lot of pain when you run out, you can contact me for a refill.

"Keep an ice pack on the area around your eye today and possibly tomorrow. That'll reduce the swelling. A bag of peas is probably the best thing to use—a bag of frozen peas. Wrap it in a towel and hold it in place for a few minutes. Remove it for a few and repeat.

"Do you have any questions?"

Daisy shook her head, so he continued, "I'd like for you to tell me what happened. Take your time."

She began, "I was just going to check on Keira. She's missing. I went to her trailer and..." Daisy rocked to and fro, as tears flooded her eyes. When she began to hyperventilate,

Dr. Thibaut took hold of her arms to stop her.

"That's enough. You don't have to talk about it now."

He asked the nurse to call in Sheriff Williams and Jake.

"I'm Dr. Thibaut," he began. "Daisy is having a tough time telling me what happened. Can you fill me in?"

Jake shook his head. "I really don't know much. Daisy called and said she'd been attacked. I told her to come here and that I'd meet her. That's it."

He thought a minute and added, "She did tell me that she'd been at the Cullasaja Gorge. When she disappeared, she'd been searching for a girl who just vanished, Keira Swan."

Daisy groaned and began to interrupt, but the doctor stopped her.

"She mentioned Keira. I'm giving you two Percocet to give her as soon as she's home, and a prescription for more. I'm also adding a prescription for Ativan, to calm her if she experiences flashbacks. I've told her to keep ice on it for the rest of today. Use a bag of frozen peas if you prefer.

"I want her to have a CT scan, but we can do that another day. When she is calmer,

"I'll fax you a copy of the exam," he said to Ben and then left before Daisy could argue. She hated all the fuss and simply wanted to get home.

They waited until a nurse returned with them. "Do you need a wheelchair?" Daisy shook her head. Jake helped Daisy to a chair in the ER waiting room while he got his car.

Once they were in the car and on the road back to her home, Jake tuned the radio to the Western Carolina University channel. A Tyler Childers song, *I'm Yourn,* was ending and immediately a man singing *Pretty Polly* began:

Oh Polly, Pretty Polly, come go along with me.
Polly, Pretty Polly, come go along with me.
Before we get married some pleasures to see.

When he turned into the driveway, Daisy woke up. The song was nearing the end, so she heard:

He stabbed her in the heart and her heart's blood did flow.
He stabbed her in the heart and her heart's blood did flow.
And into the grave Pretty Polly did go.

Daisy shuddered at the memory of why she had gone to the Swans' trailers to begin with. Keira. More than ever, she was determined to find out where Keira was. More than ever, she believed that, wherever she was, Keira was still alive.

When they reached Lucas's place, she insisted on going to her own apartment over the garage. Not wanting to upset her, Jake helped her up the stairs and into her room. After she had taken the painkillers, she said, "Thank you, Jake. Can you do one more thing for me?"

"Of course."

"Bring Rescue to me."

She was asleep when he returned with the cat. They both lay down close to Daisy and fell asleep too.

CHAPTER

19

It was the time of day when shadows failed, and all was quiet, between bird song and the trill of tree frogs, the harsh buzzing of cicadas. The gray-blue sky cast enough light to show leaves, branches, trunks, rocks, and earth that had all been painted black.

Daisy slowly woke to the realization that she was in her own bed with the small, rescued calico snuggling between her knees. As she stretched her arms above her head and straightened and stretched her legs, the cat crept from under the covers and flopped on a pillow.

"Hello, Rescue."

The small cat rolled over to show her belly for rubs. Daisy switched on the bedside lamp and took a minute to indulge her cat, then getting out of bed, she walked to the bathroom. Her left eye had swollen completely shut overnight. It and her cheek were all the colors of a rainbow.

She brushed her teeth and went to the kitchen.

In the great room she opened the refrigerator and got a can of Coke. As she popped it open, she heard a voice.

"Good morning darlin'."

Turning around, she saw Jake and recalled that he had helped her home.

"Why are you still here?"

"The doc gave you a pretty strong painkiller that knocked you out. I stayed to make sure you didn't get up in a fog and hurt yourself."

Embarrassed by her condition and her actions that led her here, she tossed out, "Well. Since you're here, why don't you take me out for dinner?"

"Dinner! Try for breakfast, and I think I can make that for you here."

As Daisy understood that she had slept through the night, the room grew brighter, and the chittering of the birds' dawn chorus began. She looked at the window which was still open. Rescue was alert on the sill and chattered in excitement at the prospect of catching a bird. Daisy walked over and scratched the cat's head. Rescue looked back annoyed, seemed to shrug her off, and returned her attention to the birds flying from tree to tree.

"Take these. Percocet." He handed her two capsules with a glass of orange juice. "You have more painkillers for later. The doc in the ER said he'd give you another prescription when you run out, or you could take extra-strength ibuprofen. It's up to you."

As toast popped up, he grated cheese on the omelet still on the stove. He folded it out on a plate and added sliced vine-ripe tomatoes. Buttered toast. Coffee. He set the breakfast on the table and grabbed a plate and a coffee for himself. "Come join me."

Jake pulled out a chair for Daisy and, once she was settled, sat down and began to eat. Both were starving and, forgetting good manners, shoveled the food in.

Daisy paused long enough to say, "Umm, good. When did you learn to cook like this?"

Jake laughed. "When you were off in Chapel Hill."

"Has Sheriff Williams come by? I need to talk with him, tell him about the cabin by the Cullasaja Gorge."

"The only thing you need to do today is to rest and recover. Ben will come by tomorrow. And no buts!"

"He needs to go to Judith Swan's trailer. That's where I was attacked."

She finished the meal in a few minutes. Putting her hand to her eye, she groaned, "At a locked door. Please tell him.

"I must look a sight."

Jake nodded.

"I wouldn't be thinking about entering any beauty contests if I were you."

He took a bag of frozen peas from the freezer, wrapped it in a hand towel, and gave it to her.

"For that lump."

She wobbled over to the couch followed closely by Jake.

"The Percocet must be taking effect," she said.

Jake supported her by taking her elbow in a firm grip. Rescue took advantage of Daisy's condition to jump on the table and clean the breakfast plates.

Jake helped her to the couch. He went to her bedroom and returned with a pillow. She stretched out with her head on the pillow and placed the frozen peas over her eyes. Jake sat at the other end of the couch and placed her feet on his lap.

"Do you want to watch TV?"

"Huh uh," she mumbled.

Jake had brought a book to read, *A Man and His Car*.

"Want me to read to you?" He held the cover for her to see.

She sniggered. "Huh uh."

Jake read silently as Daisy drifted into sleep.

CHAPTER

20

When Daisy woke again, she was in her bed, and it was clearly nighttime. The light beside her bed was on, and she checked the time on her iPhone. 11:30. On top of the covers, Rescue was sitting, watching her carefully. "Meow," she pleaded.

"I guess you're hungry," Daisy replied.

They went to the great room. Jake twisted and snorted on the couch where he lay covered with a light Afghan throw that Daisy kept for the cool mountain evenings. He turned over and went back to snoring lightly.

Daisy made a cup of coffee and gave Rescue fresh water and Friskies salmon. She glanced at the open window that overlooked the forest behind her apartment and left it open for the cat. Carrying her cup, she returned to her bed, picked up the sky-blue journal, and considered how to write about her recent experience. She took a sip of coffee and began.

RUTH MCCOY

July 9

I've been journaling since Dr. Ammons recommended it in order to "own" my feelings and to "accept" myself and my past, warts and all. But recently I hadn't been too excited about exploring either my feelings or my past, so I didn't write much until Keira Swan returned unexpectedly to Franklin with a baby.

She disappeared in the night, without the infant. Common sense says it's hers, but Keira didn't say anything about the birth or the father. She left no note to explain her disappearance. Susie Q tracked her down Wayah Road to where Keira's scent vanished, leading us to think someone in a car picked her up. No idea if she went willingly or not. Either way I have to find her.

I went to the Swans' trailer. I don't know what happened there except to say someone hit me so hard I blacked out. I guess it was one of the Swans, but I really don't know. Whoever slugged me took me in my own Jeep to what appeared to be a deserted mountain cabin and left me. There must have been another person involved to take them both back to the valley. I woke up with a black eye and a lump on the side of my face. Oh yeah, and a headache that won't quit.

Inside, the cabin was spotlessly clean, sparsely furnished, just a couple of couches. The doors to the bedrooms were locked with deadbolts. I thought about trying to break in but started worrying that whoever brought me here might return, so I left. My cell phone hadn't worked at that cabin. When I finally had reception, I called Jake, and he took over.

Jake. I've known him forever. He's building a house on his family farm. He wants me to help plan and decorate it. He wants a commitment from me, but I can't give him that.

Not yet.

"How you feeling?"

On cue Jake stood in the doorway.

"Much better," Daisy began. "I'll be ok on my own now. Your mom probably needs your help more than I do. I'll come by tomorrow. Lunchtime."

He hesitated but knew better than to argue with her. Instead, he took a bag of peas from the freezer and wrapped it in a fresh towel. Taking it to her, he said, "Have you looked in a mirror yet?"

Daisy tried to make a face at him but could only manage a weird, oddly funny half-grimace. Jake gave her the peas. He fetched a Percocet and a glass of water, then watched her down them.

"See you in the morning."

Jake left.

Daisy waited until she heard her front door open and close, then she set her journal on the nightstand, and switched off the light. She had no idea of what she would do the next day, but she knew it would begin at the Swan's trailer.

CHAPTER

21

The windshield wipers worked overtime in a futile attempt to stay ahead of the dense rain blocking her view of the road and traffic ahead. Somehow Jake had managed to bring her Jeep to the driveway while she slept, and, once again, she was going to the Hillside Mobile Home Park to find Keira's relatives, however she kept flashing back to her previous visit, which was also in a driving rain like this.

This time her bag held not only a heavy-duty Maglite, but also the Sig Sauer that Jake had taught her how to use and then helped her buy. She would not be caught off guard. She shook off the memory of waking alone, of the strange cabin high above the Cullasaja River.

Panic had not yet set in, but she was relieved when her cell sang out her new ringtone, "Good Day Sunshine."

"Daisy? We heard you're back," Retta Walker said. Her

soft, alto voice was always comforting to Daisy. "I know it's cats and dogs out there, but Louisa and I want to bring you some lunch. Okay?"

"I'd love lunch," Daisy quickly replied.

Perhaps the rain would end before afternoon, and she could continue her search for Keira.

"But I'm out now. Can I come right over?"

"Of course, dear," Retta replied. "See you soon."

Daisy was still in town and, instead of continuing south toward the trailer park, took the exit for Highway 64 West. Passing the exit her mother had taken to the deserted road where she had died, Daisy automatically turned to look. She used the next exit for Ruby Mine Road that would take her beyond the mine, the site of the small plane crash last fall, and on to Retta's mountaintop cabin.

She parked and entered the cabin without knocking. "I'm here!"

Daisy was amazed each time she entered the modern state-of-the-art home. Outside she saw a primitive log plank cabin with a stacked stone chimney. Within, only the fireplace retained the appearance of the exterior. Usually, a façade hid a poor interior, but in the case of this cabin the goal was reversed. The homely façade concealed a comfortable, modern house.

The government had looked into seizing the house as obtained with funds made through Retta's husband's illegal drug smuggling, but the investigation proved that Retta's daughter Jasmine had remodeled the cabin with her own money made in her Atlanta-based consulting business.

"Come on back. We're on the back porch enjoying the storm," Retta called out.

Unwilling to wait, Louisa Simpson came lumbering out and grabbed Daisy in a bear hug. Neither woman was that small, but Louisa used her advantage in momentum to lift Daisy off her feet.

Winded, Daisy managed to squeak, "Louisa! Put me down."

Louisa did just that but did not apologize. Putting her arm over Daisy's shoulders and shepherding her to the back of the house, she said, "Look at that face! Come on back. We got a great spread laid out for lunch. You didn't carry Jake with you?"

Daisy understood that the "spread" referred to a feast, not a bedspread, and said, "Good thing I came hungry. I didn't know Jake was invited, too."

"We just figured that you'd bring him. Seems like you're pretty close these days," Louisa said.

"He's just a friend," Daisy said.

"Mighty good friend," Louisa chortled.

Daisy shook her off and entered the screened back porch that stretched across the length of the house.

"Oh Daisy," Retta said. "We'd heard you were injured but I never..."

Daisy reached for her eye, less swollen now, but she could imagine how it must look to Retta and Louisa.

"It looks worse than it is," she said, then changing the topic she added, "But look at this! You've outdone yourselves."

The two had set up an elegant summer lunch, the kind seen at many a church meeting, on a picnic table.

To begin, a platter held turkey with cheddar cheese cubes skewered with toothpicks topped with twisted colored cellophane, followed by ham with Swiss cheese cubes done the same way. Assorted sandwich breads were on the next tray with slices of turkey and ham. Bite-sized carrots and broccoli formed a ring around a bowl of ranch dressing. Sliced cheese shared a plate with saltines. For dessert, fruit. Watermelon chunks, red and green grapes, bananas and pineapple portions speared with toothpicks, and cantaloupe sections surrounding a pottery dish of cream cheese and marshmallow dip.

"You go first," Retta said.

Daisy knew better than to argue and took one of the glass plates. She tried not to look like a glutton, but when she reached the end of the table, her plate was full to the rim. Frosty glasses of sweet tea, napkins, and silverware were already on another table. Daisy took a seat and waited for Retta and Louisa to join her.

Halfway through the meal, the two began to question her.

"We heard what happened to you. At the Swans' trailer," Retta said. "I reckon Jake already fussed at you enough for all of us."

"Actually, he was nice. I guess I scared him when I disappeared. And then when he saw me..."

Her voice trailed off as she remembered what had happened and imagined what might have happened had he not been there to take charge. In shock from the assault on her and her kidnapping and desertion on an unfamiliar road, Daisy could have lost her way and ended up in more danger.

Her voice choked as she said, "He's really my best friend in Franklin."

"There, there," Retta said. "It's over now."

"You're safe with us," Louisa chimed in.

Louisa was getting up to hug Daisy again, so she quickly collected herself and refused to cry.

"It's just too soon to talk about it."

She decided it was better not to tell them that she had been on the way to the Swans' trailers again when they called. Instead, she asked, "Has Keira come back? Has anyone heard from her?"

Louisa always kept up with local gossip and eagerly answered, "No ma'am. Not a squeak. Like she varnished into thin air."

"Louisa, settle down. Quit making such a fuss," Retta admonished. Louisa sat down.

Daisy returned to picking over her food. Her eyes had been bigger than her stomach, so she could not possibly eat everything. She ate most of the fruit and then said, "I'm more tired than I thought."

"Why don't you stretch out in the bedroom and sleep for a while?" Retta said.

"No," Daisy said. "I really need to go back home. Thank you anyway."

Louisa rose and began to fill a plate with ham, turkey, cheese, and bread. "You kin take this wi'you." She covered it with plastic wrap. "I'll carry it to your car."

Retta got up with Daisy, and they began to walk outside. They did not speak until they reached the Jeep. Then Retta said, "You know you are always welcome here. Don't be a stranger."

Daisy was about to get in, but suddenly turned and asked, "By the way, is Jasmine staying with you? I saw her at the bookstore a few days ago."

Retta tilted her head and frowned. "I guess she was too busy to stop by. Her business takes her all over the place."

Daisy nodded and said, "I still need to thank her for saving me last fall. When Christian was about to kill me.

"Thank you for everything."

Driving down Ruby Mine Road, she thought about stopping by the closed mine store where Jasmine saved her life by killing Christian, but she remembered her mission for the day: find out what happened to Keira Swan. She still thought lightning would not strike twice and assumed she would be safe at the trailer park.

CHAPTER

22

The rain had paused while Daisy was in the house, but, as she passed the old mine, it returned with a vengeance. After several years of drought on the East Coast, one storm system after another now plagued the valley. The storms came from all directions. Warm fronts from the south often carried remnants of hurricanes in the Gulf of Mexico, and from the east, vestiges of Atlantic storms. In summer, cold fronts to the west and north of the valley carried extreme weather, blasting the valley with hard rains and lightning strikes until they passed leaving cooler weather behind for a brief time.

Daisy could barely see through the rain sheeting on her windshield so, even though she was familiar with Ruby Mine Road, she crept down the mountain. She remembered how once storm water had carried her old Wrangler into a boulder and did not wish to repeat that. When she reached the highway at last, she joined traffic that moved slowly. Impatient drivers raced ahead, spraying slower cars with sheets of rain, but Daisy was content to go with the flow.

She realized that going down to the trailer park in this storm was not a promising idea. Instead, she drove to the sheriff's office to ask Ben Williams for an update on the search for Keira. In the parking lot, she saw several cars. One she recognized as belonging to the chief of police for Franklin. One she did not recognize bore Georgia plates.

Juanita Williams, Ben's wife who was also his administrative assistant, took one look at her and said, "You oughta be in bed."

To forestall more comments about her eye, she said, "Looks worse than it is. I'd like to see Ben to ask about Keira."

"Not possible. He's been in a meeting most of the day, and I think he'll be busy all afternoon. He just had me get them carryout from the new Chick-fil-A near Walmart."

"Who's in there besides the Chief? Someone from Atlanta?"

"You guessed it. Mr. FBI." Juanita studied Daisy's face for her reaction. Nathan Stark seemed interested in knowing Daisy better last fall, and Daisy seemed to reciprocate.

She saw Daisy only nodding her head until she said, "I see. I see. Do you think I could wait?"

"Pointless unless you want to waste an afternoon."

"They're meeting about Keira, aren't they? Do they have any leads?"

She knew that Daisy was desperate for news, that she felt partially responsible for Keira's disappearance.

"If I knew something, I promise I'd tell you, but they

aren't even letting me in on what they're doing. I promise you."

"You'll call me if you learn anything?"

"Sure thing."

CHAPTER

23

Daisy rushed through the rain to her Jeep. She might not have learned the specifics of the meeting in the sheriff's office, but she was smart enough to realize that Keira's disappearance and the reason she left her baby with Lexie and Brad was worse than she had imagined, that most likely Keira's kin were not involved. It was something more sinister.

The rain showed no signs of stopping. She took the Old Murphy Road toward Jake's farm. He would be pleased to see she had not gone in search of more trouble. He might let her use his computer to do more research. She also hoped he would use his advanced skills to do a more thorough search. Perhaps into the Dark Web. Maybe she could find similar disappearances in Macon County. She was not one to let a lead go until she had traced it to the source, and since the rise of social media, the internet was an important research tool.

Just before she reached the dollar store, she saw flashing lights ahead. As she drew closer, there was a barricade and signs pointing to a detour to 64. A deputy used a flashlight to motion the way to go. This area was often the first to flood in heavy rains. The dollar store once had to close for months to repair flood damage, and the manager hoped repairs would prevent flood waters from creeping inside. This would be the first test since work had been completed.

On the highway, traffic was creeping along with the usual drivers making fools of themselves speeding. At least one was sure to cause accidents farther down the road.

Daisy stayed with the tortoises, but soon reached the exit for Old Wayah Road. The farm road which crossed the Cartoogechaye Creek also flooded but never enough to be impassable. She turned into the road and easily drove through the low flood.

Unlike the road by the dollar store which needed only heavy rain to flood, the road to the farmhouse had room for the flood waters to spread out. The water did not reach the floor of the Jeep. She drove cautiously, but she knew the road well enough to keep to it. Finally reaching the house, she saw Susie Q on the front porch. She was already wagging her tail, but not barking. Daisy turned off the car and raced through the storm to reach her.

"Down, Susie Q," she said. The redbone hound obeyed and sat until Daisy opened the front door. Then she bounded past her leaping with excitement but not touching Daisy.

"Clemmie," Daisy called out. "It's Daisy."

"Come on back, dear," Clemmie answered. "What are you doing out on a day like this?

Daisy laughed. "That is just what I have been asking myself. For your information, it looks worse than it is."

She stopped as she entered the kitchen. Clemmie had dragged a chair from the porch and sat rocking the baby. Susie Q now sat with her chin resting on Clemmie's knee to complete the tableau. She imagined the same scenario when Jake was a baby.

"Go dry yourself off."

Daisy went to the guest room she occupied when she visited. The soft robe was hanging on a hook and a pair of slippers were by the bed. She quickly changed into them and went to the kitchen where Jake's mother had prepared a cup of hot chocolate for them. The baby, swaddled in a soft cotton blanket, slept in a small wooden cradle on the table.

As they settled to drink the hot chocolate, Clemmie said, "I guess you know you should be in bed."

Daisy ignored the remark.

"Well. I've been chasing my tail all day."

She blew on the hot chocolate to cool it.

"It started out okay — except for the rain. I'd planned to go back to the Swans' trailers to see if they had heard yet from Keira, but Retta called and invited me for lunch. The sky opened up just as I was leaving.

"I got drenched when I went to the sheriff's office to see what Ben knew. He was in a meeting with the Franklin Chief of Police and that FBI agent from last year. Juanita wouldn't let me interrupt them. Orders from the sheriff.

"The storm hasn't stopped yet."

Daisy told Clemmie about the flooded road by the Family Dollar Store and the detour.

"I'm hoping Jake will let me use his computer—and maybe help me look for other missing babies in the area."

"Of course he will, dear. You rest now, and I'll give him a call to let him know you're here. I'll wash and dry your clothes, too."

Relieved that Clemmie was taking charge, Daisy began to go. Before leaving, she turned to say, "I'm so glad little Lexie is with you."

CHAPTER

24

Susie Q barked furiously at a muddy puddle of water. Daisy shouted at her to stop, but the hound kept on barking. When Daisy went to grab her collar, the long-legged hound turned and said, "A great flood is coming. Build a raft and put your whole family on it, and you all will be saved. White caps formed on the water, and the raft swayed violently beneath her. If you don't..."

Jake was leaning over Daisy and shaking her awake. She had fallen asleep on the couch.

"I must've been dreaming. Has it stopped raining?"

Jake sat beside her and said, "Nope. It's supposed to rain like this pretty much all week."

Moaning in disappointment, she said, "I've got so much to do."

"I hope you don't mean too much to do in tracking

down Keira. You've already seen how dangerous that is."

Daisy did not acknowledge that statement. She changed the subject and said, "I've decided to search online instead of on the mountains. Can you help?"

"Of course, darlin', but first," he said as he gave her more frozen peas. After she held it to her eye, he said, "What do you need me to do?"

Daisy explained that she wanted to search for other missing babies in Macon County.

"Sure thing. At least I'll be able to keep my eye on you. Let's go to my office."

In one of the bedrooms upstairs Jake had run cables to access the internet on a desktop computer. The desk faced one window, and a comfortable armchair had been placed under the other. A wall of bookshelves held books about computing, architecture, and interior design, accounting logbooks, and a vast collection of fiction.

Jake sat down and turned on the computer. When the bootup was completed, he opened the browser and entered the keywords "Abandoned babies in Macon County North Carolina." In seconds, a list of sites referenced to Keira and her baby. No other infants were reported as missing.

One site led to a news story about the North Carolina Safe Surrender Law which since 2007 let new mothers leave their babies with adults without being charged with abandonment. It applies to newborns up to seven days old, and the adult must be a responsible caretaker.

"I wonder if that applies to Keira. Did she say when the baby was born?" Daisy said. "I guess I'll have to ask Lexie."

Jake scrolled down but found no other cases. He went through several pages before giving up.

"I don't think there have been any more reported."

"Can you check Atlanta?"

The first page of the search results had links to three newborns, including one left on a porch with the umbilical cord still attached. There was also a link to the Georgia Safe Place for Newborns Act of 2002, which was the same as the North Carolina law.

Daisy read each article. "These don't seem to be the same as Keira's situation. I wish Ben would tell me what's going on."

"Daisy, you promised not to keep looking on your own," Jake said. "I'm going to hold you to that."

"All right! Can you look at the Dark Web to see what we can find?"

"After supper. You forget I've been working all day."

Downstairs Clemmie had already set the table and was getting a casserole dish from the oven. She placed it carefully on a brass trivet in the center of the table beside a basket of hot rolls wrapped in a napkin.

"Help yourselves," she said as she sat down and put her napkin on her lap. "It's my Chicken Spectacular."

She did not need to name the dish because it was both Jake's and Daisy's favorite. Daisy thought the crunchy water chestnuts made it "spectacular." Their glasses were already filled with sweet tea, and a full pitcher completed the table. Families in the valley had different methods of making the brew. Daisy used Clemmie's system which she liked for its simplicity. Using a special teapot, she first added an eyeballed amount of white sugar. Next, she dangled a family-sized tea bag over the edge, poured boiling water into the pot, stirred vigorously, and left it alone until the water reached the color she was looking for. Then she poured the tea over a special pitcher filled with ice and ended up with a perfect sweet tea without fail.

"How's your work coming along? I mean, on the computer," Clemmie asked.

Jake did not answer so Daisy replied, "Not very well. Jake searched all of Macon County and then in Atlanta but didn't find anything like Keira and her baby. After we eat, we're going..."

She stopped when Jake kicked her under the table. Looking at him, she saw him shaking his head, and he took over saying, "We'll search some more."

"I've been thinking, and it's not exactly the same, but it must have been around 1985 or 86." Clemmie was thinking out loud. "You know Gladys Sommers, from the Garden Club. Her daughter, Betty, was pregnant, not married. That happened quite a lot in those days. One day she packed a small bag, left Franklin, and never returned.

"Her mother hadn't chastised or been mean to her. We never could figure out why she would do that. Just leave."

Daisy and Jake helped clear the table and returned to his office.

"I want to see if I can find anything about the girl Mom mentioned. What was her name?? Beth"

"Betty," Daisy said. "I hope we can find Keira."

She looked out the window at the pouring rain. It had stalled her search and she was eager to resume it again.

Jake said, "Nothing. Just an obituary for Gladys Sommers. Nothing interesting about a Betty Sommers."

"Did you try the newspaper archives?"

"No, why don't you scroll through them and see what you can find?"

Thirty minutes of Daisy's online search found nothing more. Jake took over the computer. He shut it down, rebooted it, and opened a new window. Only moments later, a screen appeared—Duck Duck Go. Daisy tried to scrunch her face at Jake.

"You remember how I set up a 'ghost VPN' on your laptop so you could do research for your articles?" Jake said. "Your search history wasn't saved so no one could tell where you had been or what you were looking for."

"Yeah."

"Well, this site takes a giant step ahead. Look at the address. '.onion' signifies that this version of Duck Duck Go is on Tor, in the Dark Web. It's like putting a surgical dressing over a band aid."

"But Tor. Isn't that a place for criminals? Pushers and thieves? And..."

"Kidnappers," Jake finished. "We can't find Keira anywhere else, so we'll search here. What should we search for first?"

"Keira, I guess. Keira."

Jake typed her name in the new browser. Daisy drew in closer to the screen as the new page filled with sites mentioning "Keira." She pointed to a site. "Open that one."

"Keira is a Gaelic name meaning black, or little dark one," she read. "See Ciaran."

Other sites lead to the same--the meaning of the name. Still others mentioned Keira Knightley and other people Daisy was not familiar with. Jake went to the next page and found the same results.

"Try her whole name."

Jake went back to the browser and entered "Keira Swan." A wealth of new links opened. They all seemed to mention Keira as a member of the "Swan Family," a criminal organization.

"Pooh," Daisy said. "If the Swans are a criminal organization, then I'm the Queen of England. Can you type in "Swan Family" to see what's there?"

Many links to swans appeared—one with a list of the seven types of swans worldwide. Another stating that the Queen does own all unmarked mute swans found in open waters in the United Kingdom.

Finally, a link to the Swans of North Carolina appeared. Daisy held her breath as Jake clicked on the link.

Daisy read out loud, "The Swans have been involved in bootlegging since the Prohibition experiment in the 1920s when George Arthur Swan began to sell moonshine in Macon County."

She paused to say, "That must be Keira's great-grandfather."

Jake summarized the rest, "It goes on to say how their involvement in bootlegging changed over the years. They used their stills to keep the area supplied with moonshine. When Prohibition ended, they smuggled liquor to avoid paying the stamp tax. Gradually they moved into drugs and found that to be more lucrative than liquor."

Daisy blurted out, "We already knew all that. Does it mention infants? Or kidnapping?"

Jake shook his head. Daisy wrapped her arms around herself. Not from cold. From fear that they would not find anything that could help her find Keira.

"Can you search for something else? Kidnapping adults, for example?"

Jake said, "Daisy, you don't understand how the dark web works. There are hundreds of sites to search. There are other search engines in the Dark Web. We have barely scratched the surface."

"I can't just stand here, doing nothing. It drives me crazy."

"I don't have to tell you that you don't always get what you want. Especially without hard work."

Daisy paced around the small office, turned to Jake, and said, "You don't want me to go looking by myself. How about you coming with me? We could go back to the cabin I was taken to. Or to the Swans' trailers at the Hillside Mobile Home Park?"

"Can you wait until tomorrow?"

"If it means you'll come with me."

Clemmie insisted that Daisy stay the night. She called Lucas to let him know. Then they settled down to watch TV before going to bed.

As Daisy lay in bed, her thoughts returned to the strange dream she had about a flood. And being rescued by Susie Q. The redbone hound had followed Keira's trail once before, to the spot where it simply vanished. Probably because Keira had gotten into a car.

Did she get in the car of her own free will? Had she been kidnapped? Why would she leave her newborn baby with Lexie and Brad? How can I find her?

CHAPTER

25

Dawn came and went. Heavy clouds and pounding rain had concealed it, and the storm promised to last all day. When Daisy awoke, Jake had already left for work at Drake.

"He said to stay put," Clemmie told her as she poured fresh hot coffee and set a plate of warm angel biscuits on the oak table. "I just made these, so sit down and eat before they get cold."

Daisy split a biscuit in two. She slathered it with butter and then piled on strawberry preserves that Clemmie had canned in June. "Um, good," she said with a mouth full of biscuit.

"There's more if you want them."

Daisy scarfed down the two that remained on her plate and took a sip of coffee.

"Did Jake say when he'd get back?'

"He said he'd be here by lunch, so I figure it'll be in one or two hours."

"What time is it?"

"Just a little after ten. I thought you needed more rest and let you sleep in."

Daisy returned to the guest room to shower and dress for the day. The swelling had gone down, and her black eye had turned more green and yellow than black. Clemmie had laundered her clothes and laid them out while she was eating. When she returned to the kitchen, Clemmie was nowhere to be seen.

Daisy went up to Jake's office. His desktop computer had been shut down. She left it alone and looked at the wall of books. They were neatly arranged by subject matter first and then alphabetized. Her own things were always in such a mess that she was impressed. A section that held map books caught her eye. She drew close and ran her finger along the spines until she pulled one out, Macon County, North Carolina.

Sitting down in the armchair under the window, she opened it. Franklin was in the center of the first page which contained a map of the whole county. She flipped through until she came to a double page showing the area around the Cullasaja Gap. She found no sign of the road leading to the cabin which she had been taken to. Impossible! She gathered all the books for the area and carried them to Jake's desk. She found the road, marked with a dotted line on a map for use by the National Forest Service.

She returned to the bookshelves and selected one provided by the U.S. Department of Agriculture titled *Fire Management*. The amount of information was overwhelming, but she picked through the chapter headings to clarify in her mind the reasons for different fire control measures.

Roads, such as the one she had woken up in, provided access to remote areas and allowed the Service to monitor wildfire prevention strategies and for Fire Fighters to reach fires in the mountains. Selective cutting could provide fire breaks that wildfires cannot jump across. Strip cutting at a right angle to winds could halt wind-driven fires. Prescribed, or controlled, fires could clear out highly combustible undergrowth which burns slower than fires along the treetops, but which are much more difficult to control.

Daisy took the books and returned downstairs. She looked outside at the rain still falling. It was then she noticed her car and on a small table by the door saw her keys. She sought out Clemmie to thank her for the TLC.

"Are you sure you don't want to rest here a while longer?"

"It's appealing, but I need to get home," Daisy replied. Seeing the concerned look on Clemmie's face, she added, "I promise I'll go straight home."

Clemmie smiled and hugged her. "You know you're welcome here anytime."

Daisy was as good as her word and went straight to her apartment over the garage. She made two phone calls: one to Ed asking him to bring Rescue home, and one to Jake telling him that she was getting ready to return to the isolated cabin—with or without him.

CHAPTER

26

Rescue lounged on her back with her head wedged between a pillow and the back of the couch in Daisy's great room. Next to her, Daisy was eating a grilled cheese sandwich and drinking a Coke from a plastic bottle. The TV was tuned to the Weather Channel. Home for less than an hour, the two were settling quickly into the routine they had followed before Keira disappeared. Daisy lazily scratched the calico's furry stomach as she ate and watched.

"I wish I could bring better news for the East Coast," Stephanie Abrams said sprightly with a smile on her face, "but I'm afraid you're in for more of the same for the rest of the week. The problem is...," she said as she turned to the map, "...that you have a warm front that has stalled over Atlanta, Western North Carolina, Tennessee, and Virginia. It is slowly moving up the Appalachian Mountains to the

Northeast."

Daisy switched off the weather report and continued to eat and gently rub Rescue's stomach. Suddenly Rescue jumped up to the back of the sofa where she slouched and licked her belly and her legs as she stretched them out one by one. She resembled an old lady who, upon being caught in spreading gossip, true or not, smoothed her clothes, adjusted her handbag, and looked around as if to say, "Humph, what you think doesn't bother me in the least."

Daisy finished her sandwich at the same time as Rescue ended her grooming, and they went their separate ways. Daisy to shower and Rescue to gaze out the window, now closed against the storm.

Dressed and ready to go, she took out her laptop. She entered "babies" and watched as multiple entries rolled by. Many sites were dedicated to providing various advice on caring for babies and toddlers, stages of physical and mental development, and links to funny videos of babies playing with animals. Daisy opened a link to a news report about the black market for babies in the United States. She scanned the article from the *Atlanta Journal-Constitution* which described how babies were stolen from hospital nurseries, taken to adoption centers, and sold to couples, usually older, who were desperate to have a child of their own. The agencies collected upwards of $50,000 for an infant.

That isn't the case with Keira. Baby Alexa isn't missing. Keira is.

She was deep in thought when Jake knocked on the door and backed into the room without waiting for a response. He was shaking and closing a large umbrella behind him. Daisy closed her laptop.

Rescue jumped down from the window and sped to welcome Jake by entwining herself around his ankles. He placed the umbrella by the door and picked up the petite cat.

"How's Miss Rescue doin' today?" he said as he rubbed the top of her head. Rescue purred.

Daisy pretended to pout. "What about me? I'm the one who was nearly killed a few days ago."

Jake laughed and slowly looked her up, down, and up again.

"You're lookin' just fine to me."

If Daisy were the blushing type, her cheeks would have turned bright pink.

"Except for that eye," he added.

"Stop it, Jacob Smith! Are you ready to go?"

He put Rescue down and grabbed his umbrella. Daisy got a raincoat with a hood, her bag, the map book she had brought from Jake's house, and her iPhone. They set out to find the mysterious trailer where Daisy had found herself after being assaulted at the Swans'.

CHAPTER

27

The tempest swirled around them. Daisy usually feared having a panic attack on dirt-and-gravel roads in rainstorms, but she felt secure with Jake in his four-wheel-drive. She had made an appointment with her therapist Dr. Ammons, but that was for the next week. She flinched as the truck hit a pothole.

"Not to worry," Jake said. "I'm in control here. Won't let anything happen to you."

Last fall Daisy would have frozen at those words and would have chewed him out for daring to presume that she needed his help for anything. Today, however, as they drew nearer to the isolated cabin, his presence reassured her. The closer they got, the more she dreaded learning what they would find.

Jake pulled into the driveway, overgrown with weeds and small brushes, of the dilapidated cabin. Turning off the engine, he faced Daisy. She was breathing faster and had not unbuckled her seat belt.

"How're you doing?"

She did not answer. "Do you want to wait here while I check it out?"

Daisy shook her head. "No, I need to see this."

Jake waited as she made her way around the front of the truck, and they walked to the weather-worn front door. Jake knocked with the butt of the large flashlight he carried. As before, no one answered. He turned the knob and nudged the door open.

The room seemed much the same as on Daisy's prior visit except that, close to the door where the large blue sectional couch and loveseat should have sat, nothing. Across the large room was the kitchen. Daisy went ahead. The countertops and sink were still spotless. She opened the refrigerator. It was empty. The case of Dasani was gone.

"Someone has been here. There was a large flat of bottled water, and it's gone." She opened the cabinets, one by one. Again, they were empty. "They've taken everything."

Jake tried the light switch, but the cabin remained in the dark. He turned on the flashlight. "Wait here," he said as he entered the dark hall.

"I don't want to be alone," she said and followed close behind him. "The first door is the bathroom."

Jake opened the door, peered in, and left it open. Next were bedrooms that were unlocked and held nothing. When they approached the last door, he tried the doorknob which turned easily, so he shoved the door open. He took a step into the room and shone the light around.

"Wait here," he said. For once she listened as he crossed

the room and opened another door. He returned to the hallway.

"Nothing."

"That can't be," Daisy exclaimed. "It had to have contained something important."

Taking his flashlight, she pushed ahead and saw for herself the empty room.

"I don't understand," she said at last.

Jake crossed and opened the shades covering the windows to allow for more light. He studied the room for signs that it had been occupied. He knelt at a spot and felt the wood.

"Something heavy was here. Someone dragged it for a while. See?"

She looked where he pointed.

"I think that here," he said pointing to the spot where the gouge marks in the pine floor ended, "they either picked it up or put it on a dolly. You were right."

No one had cleaned the floor when they cleared out the equipment, and bare patterns in the dust revealed where other things had been positioned. A strap on his shoulder held a small digital camera which he took and began taking photos of the room.

Daisy went back to the great room and opened the curtains and shades. Walking around the room once more, she said to herself, "They even took the dish drainer and rubber mat. It's like they want us to think they had never been here. That Keira had never been here. What the heck are they doing?"

CHAPTER

28

The storm worsened as Jake drove Daisy home. Rain pounded his truck in a barrage of heavy-duty drops before pouring on sheets of water that clouded visibility and reduced traffic to a standstill. He put on his flashers and crawled along. When they reached the driveway that separated the garage and the stairs to her apartment from Lucas's house, he said, "Are you going back to your place or to Lucas's?'

"Home. That means my apartment," she said. "I left Rescue there and, if Ed came and got her, he'll just have to trot her back over."

"Do you want company?"

She unfastened her seatbelt, opened the door, and shook her head as she got out.

"But thanks for your help today. Tomorrow, can we search more on the internet?"

"Sure thing."

He continued to watch as she pulled the slicker's hood over her head and raced up the stairs. Once she disappeared inside, he left.

Daisy was drenched from her waist down. Rescue rushed from the bedroom to greet her but pulled back when she felt the wet jeans. She leapt to the back of the sofa, stretched her legs, and, ignoring Daisy, began preening.

Daisy ignored the cat in return.

She shed her slicker at the entry and went straight to her bathroom. Leaving her clothes on the floor she showered and washed her hair.

Clad in a favorite UNC basketball t-shirt, she turned on the light by her bed and propped up to read the entry she had made about Keira. She had written about Keira's surprising appearance with a baby and her shocking disappearance in the night. Attempting to track her down, Daisy had gone to the Swans' trailers south of Franklin. She remembered how she had been attacked and kidnapped, driven away in her Jeep, and left by the mysterious cabin near the Cullasaja Gorge. *Why there*? That cabin had raised more questions about Keira and increased Daisy's determination to find out what had happened.

Her calico cat jumped on the bed and burrowed under the covers next to her. Daisy reached under to scratch her head and then returned to the journal entry and began to write.

QUESTIONS:

Why had she been taken to that cabin?

Did someone abduct her and take her there to learn more about Keira's disappearance?

Why?

Who had removed everything from the cabin? Why?

Why were Ben, the Chief of Police, and Nathan Stark meeting in secret?

Had her mother ever been to that cabin? Did it have anything to do with her accident?

Could she learn anything from the newspaper article about missing babies?

As usual her thoughts returned to her mother. Daisy still believed that the accident could have been faked, and she was more determined than ever to discover the truth. She turned off her light.

Tomorrow I'll go corner Ben to find out what he has been doing with the agent and the Chief.

CHAPTER

29

When the noise of rain pounding on the roof woke Daisy up, her first thought was that it was still nighttime. Darkness enveloped her apartment over the garage. Rescue was asleep, snuggled under the covers by her legs.

She rolled to her stomach and shut her eyes. In doing so, she roused the little calico who crawled from undercover and began preening on the pillow beside Daisy. Daisy groaned and reached over her head to shove Rescue who stopped licking herself for only a beat and then resumed with even more furious licking, biting on herself, and stretching out her own legs to shove back at Daisy.

"I give up."

Without raising her head, she reached for her phone. Almost eleven. Services would be starting at the First Methodist Church, but she doubted many would be in attendance. With such heavy rainfall most Franklinites would opt to watch the service on TV in the comfort of their living rooms. She quickly showered and pulled on jeans and a loose dark blue sweatshirt.

After setting up her Keurig with a Dunkin' coffee pod, she turned on the Weather Channel. By the time her coffee was ready, Jen Carfagno was discussing the storm's progress. Clad in her familiar Weather Channel blue slicker, she was in front of the Atlanta building where the tropical storm swirled around her.

"So all I can tell you now is, if you are in the Southeast, hunker down today. Believe me, you do not want to be out in this. There will be sunshine tomorrow and Tuesday until evening when remnants of the tropical storm will pass through. It's going to be a long week of bad weather, folks."

If Daisy hated anything, it was a loss of momentum in an investigation. She was like a hound with a scent coming suddenly to a creek. Frustrated she took out her journal to review her thoughts. The last question she posed led her back to the Atlanta paper.

She thought about the article from the *Atlanta Journal-Constitution* about babies being stolen from hospital nurseries, taken to adoption centers, and sold to desperate couples who were unable to have a child. The agencies collected upwards of $50,000 for an infant.

Initially she had discarded that idea because the baby was not missing. Keira was. The question that remained was whether Keira had been abducted or had abandoned the baby. Recent events caused Daisy to think abduction was the answer. Why else would someone go to such lengths to hinder her search?

Reckoning that her dad could help her think through her questions, she put on a hoodie, put her journal in one of the pockets, pulled the hood over her head, and left Rescue to guard the apartment.

CHAPTER

30

Lucas and Ed were eating lunch on TV trays while watching CNN where the news focused on the storm.

"You're looking a lot better today," Lucas said. "Does it still hurt?"

"Looks worse than it is."

"Make yourself a sandwich and come join us," he said. "There's some bouillon still hot on the stove if you want a French dip."

She could not remember the last time she ate, so a French dip sounded like a great idea. The makings for an American-style French dip were still on the kitchen counter: Pepperidge Farm Hoagie Rolls, Dietz & Watson Sliced Roast Beef, and, peculiar to her family Duke's Mayonnaise. She assembled the sandwich and filled a bowl with the still hot bouillon.

Ed had set out a TV tray. She sat, dipped, and took an

extra-large bite of the sandwich. The juice dribbled down her chin. She wiped with the back of her hand and mumbled with a full mouth, "(unintelligible)."

"Don't talk with your mouth full," Lucas admonished.

She grunted in affirmation.

The CNN meteorologist was calmly ending his report making the storm they were enduring sound like the proverbial tempest in a teapot. Lucas remotely turned off the television.

"What brings you out in this storm—besides hunger?"

She put down her sandwich and used the napkin Ed had provided to wipe her hands and mouth. Taking her journal from her pocket, she read off the questions.

"I'm stumped. The only thing I'm pretty sure of is that her family isn't involved. They're all proud of Keira, and besides it's not their style."

"That may well be," Lucas said. "Have you considered that whoever is responsible could be more dangerous than the Swans? That should give you pause for thought."

Daisy groaned.

"That's why I'm here, Daddy. The only person I can think of is Jasmine Walker..."

"Daisy!" Lucas rebuked her.

"I know. I know, but bad things happen whenever she's in town," she said and then added, "It seems to me."

"Do you have any proof? Anything concrete, or just your suspicions?"

"Do you ever realize how annoying you can be? I'm not on the witness stand."

Daisy glared at him but then her look softened.

"I'll be careful, Daddy. I promise."

CHAPTER

31

The fact that Ben Williams was out when Daisy entered his office suited her just fine. She frequently learned more from Juanita than she did from him. Somehow, she always knew not only everything happening in the Sheriff's office, but also everything in the town.

"Morning, Juanita," Daisy said. Not one to shy away from bluntness, she continued, "What was Ben doing holed up with those men yesterday?"

"You know I'd tell you if I knew. Ben has kept me in the dark," Juanita scowled. "They usually meet up to plan raids on drug dealers, but I'm wondering if this time they were discussing Keira. Everybody's so worked up about her. Especially after what's happened to you."

"Do you think..."

"Not an idea. I would tell you if I knew," she paused, then teased, "I can tell you that Nathan Stark is the FBI agent in the group."

Daisy's brain flew to ideas about how to get the information she needed from Nathan. "I'd already figured that out. Do you know where he's staying?"

"That I can tell you. The Hampton Inn."

Daisy was about to track Nathan down when Ben walked in.

"You're looking a whole lot better. How're you feeling?"

"Back to normal," she said and then launched into her questions. "What's Nathan Stark doing in town? Is he here about Keira? Have you learned anything?'

"Whoa. Wait a minute! I guess Juanita told you."

He glared at his wife.

"That's beside the point. What can you tell me about Keira?"

Ben led her into his office and motioned for her to sit down.

"We don't have any news yet," he said. "I promise I'll tell you when we do."

Daisy believed him. Ben had never lied to her in all the time she had known him. She thought about asking him the purpose of their meeting but did not want to sidetrack herself. Instead, she told him about her return to the Cullasaja cabin with Jake. About the mysterious disappearance of all the furnishings, such as they were. About the strange gouges on the floor of the last room. About the impressions left in the dust of that room. When she finished, he shook his head.

"I'm going to have to speak to Jake. You could've gotten into serious trouble."

"I made him go. I was going to go without him if he wouldn't go with me," Daisy paused. "I think you should go up there to check it out and maybe get those FBI forensic guys to go with you. I'd like to go with you. I'm really scared that something bad happened to Keira up there."

"Look Daisy. I know how to do my job, but I promise we'll do that," he said. "If you promise me you'll quit investigating on your own, you can come tomorrow. Okay?"

"I swear. I actually have to go to work now."

"Work is okay, but then home. Deal?" Ben asked.

"Deal."

CHAPTER

32

The office was quiet for a change. The weekly newspaper's reporters were out conducting interviews for their stories. They all had regular assignments. The Chamber of Commerce was an important source of information about local businesses. Organizations like the Rotary Club, the Lions Club, and Kiwanis could always be counted on for at least a photo and lengthy cutline.

Town and county law enforcement and fire departments were tapped for regular crime and fire reports. Then there were the several historical societies covering everything from kilts to rubies to local history. The Macon County Board of Education along with the principals of individual schools were frequently called on for incidents at local schools and for future plans for curriculum and infrastructure.

Daisy's assignment had always been the Board of

Education and the schools. It occurred to her that Keira's teachers might be able to tell her more about Keira, information that could help find her. But that would have to wait.

A lone copyeditor, who did not seem to know touch typing, had mastered the hunt-and-peck method. She was rapidly firing off sections of an article with occasional stops to correct a misfire and find the necessary keys.

Daisy waved to her when she looked up and then proceeded to the editor-in-chief's office. Chad Melbourne was on the phone but nodded for her to sit down.

"It's nice to see you looking well," Chad said. Daisy's shiner had faded to a faint yellow that she no longer attempted to conceal with makeup. "I've been wanting to talk to you. But you must need something?"

"I do. You know Keira Swan is still missing, and I'm very worried about her," she began. "I have my suspicions about what's happened to her."

"Now, Daisy," Chad said, "this story is especially important, but you need to pull back. Let Ben and his crew find out what's happened to Keira."

Frustrated, Daisy shook her head. "I'm being careful. I'm not going off alone and half-cocked. Listen.

"Jake and I went back to the cabin I'd been taken to. We found it, but everything was different. All the furniture had been removed. In a room that had been locked there were signs of heavy equipment. The floor had been gouged out where something heavy was dragged."

"All right," Chad interrupted. "That's enough. That's what I'm talking about. What if Jake had been hurt? That's happened before, you know."

Daisy shuddered as she remembered the moment Jake had been wounded while helping her last fall.

"I know you're right. I've told Ben everything."

"Good!" Chad said. "Now I want you to follow up with Ben. We can do brief updates daily to keep Keira top-of-mind. I want you to talk to her friends and former classmates and come up with a human-interest story. That might jog peoples' memories. Make them recall seeing Keira that could shed light on what's happened with her."

Daisy sat at one of the office desktops and opened Google. She typed in Gladys Sommers and found a link to her obituary. Betty was mentioned among her survivors. A search for Betty Sommers revealed links to people with that name, but there was no mention of any disappearance. She copied the contact information for a Betty Sommers in Atlanta.

After writing a brief profile of Keira, she emailed it along with a photo to Chad. Then she cleared Google and typed in "Jasmine Walker."

A page filled rapidly with links to her business page and information about her years at UNC where she was head cheerleader and homecoming queen. There was much more. It was a lot to take in, but the one thing Daisy realized was that there was nothing that pointed to criminal activities.

Daisy had hardly noticed the weather when driving around earlier. As she left the newspaper office, she realized that the storm winds had lessened and scattered rain had dwindled. She also realized how tired she was. She drove home and went straight to sleep until the following day.

CHAPTER

33

The new day shined itself into Franklin with a loosely formed eye of the storm, promising calm but bound to bring a flood of terrifying knowledge which Daisy both needed and dreaded. She had been up for hours.

Seated on the couch with a second cup of coffee and her laptop, she continued surfing the internet in the hope that new information about missing women would rise to the surface above the vast sea of entries. She was now searching farther afield into Georgia and north toward Asheville. Several references to women came up, but when she looked deeper, none mentioned mothers who went missing with their infants.

When a link led to a Facebook appeal for information about a young pregnant woman, Alice McDowell, who had gone missing in February, she copied the phone number. Over a hundred comments from people, who claimed to have seen her, appeared until the settings turned comments off. Too early to make the phone call, she continued to scroll.

Impatient as usual, Daisy glanced at the time displayed on the laptop's screen. Close enough to eight for her to head out. The previous day, she had gone to the Sheriff's office and convinced Ben to let her accompany him as teams carried out a forensic search of the cabin and the surrounding area.

Almost everything she knew about forensics came from Karin Slaughter mysteries about Dr. Sara Linton and FBI Agent Will Trent. The books were set in and near Atlanta, with Grady Memorial Hospital featuring prominently.

Daisy had also read *The Body Farm* by Patricia Cornwell with graphic descriptions of bodies in various stages of decomposition. She hoped the search today would not lead to similar discoveries.

Rescue padded softly from the bedroom and lapped up water from her bowl. She sat and stared at Daisy, no doubt to remind her that she should be fed before Daisy left. She put out fresh water and kibble. She grabbed her bag and left.

Clouds stretched in a low blanket above the rivers and creeks in the valley, lending a sense of mystery to the scene. Although Daisy had always known which creeks and rivers lay under the clouds, as a young girl she had imagined they concealed monsters, like Nessie, the creature in Loch Ness in Scotland. Or the ghosts of miners in past centuries panning for gold and killing other miners, more successful at finding gold nuggets, to steal their stakes.

She also imagined the early Cherokee living, farming, and hunting peacefully until white settlers coveted their land, pushed them into the hills, and ultimately forced many to follow the Trail of Tears to the West. She had heard stories passed down through generations of the Cherokee who hid or escaped and who formed the Eastern Band of Cherokee Indians.

Having decided it best not to tell Jake of her plans to observe the forensic search, she drove alone to the remote cabin where she had been abandoned. She did not like concealing it from him, but she also did not want him to discourage her or to insist on coming along. Her confidence had been shaken and she was keen to get it back.

The road was blocked off with yellow crime scene tape. On the other side Daisy saw Sheriff Ben Williams standing with Special Agent Nathan Stark. Forensic teams had donned white plastic coveralls and were entering the cabin to gather evidence, and field agents wearing blue FBI jackets had begun to comb the area surrounding the cabin. Depending on their training, several canine units using German Shepherds had fanned out to seek either trails or corpses.

Just as Daisy crossed under the yellow tape and walked toward Ben and Nathan, one of the handlers of a cadaver dog motioned for them to approach. His dog was sitting quietly by the smokehouse.

Nathan called one of the forensic specialists to look inside the small log structure. The specialist entered the smokehouse. Then he held the door open for Nathan to see. Nathan's shoulders sank and his head bowed as he walked to where Ben and now Daisy were waiting.

"It's human remains. A skeleton. The skull is intact with its teeth so we should be able to identify it."

CHAPTER

34

The smokehouse was a small edifice built with log planks to both cure and to store ham, bacon, and other meats from a slaughtered hog. Fish could be cured as well, but not on this homestead high in the Smoky Mountains.

Smoke would pour out through vents on the roof, and a locked door would allow entry to place or retrieve the meat. No windows. In the middle of a packed dirt floor, a fire pit had held slow-burning hardwoods. The hams and other pork products were hung from the rafters to prevent rats and other woodland creatures from eating them.

Long abandoned, this smokehouse was a perfect place to conceal a crime.

"Seal this off, and the surrounding area," Ben said to a deputy carrying the crime scene tape.

From the woods below came another call, "Find." The

signal used when a cadaver dog sat or lay down when it smelled decaying remains. The dogs had been trained to distinguish between human corpses and the remains of an animal.

When Ben, Nathan, and other members of the team moved on, Daisy walked over to peer into the smokehouse. She snapped a photo of the skeleton with her cell and emailed it to herself. As she neared the search team, a series of calls echoed from the mountainside.

She sidled up to Nathan and touched him on the shoulder. "What's going on?"

Nathan took her arm and guided her to the road and her car. She did not resist. He opened the door of her Jeep and, when she was in the driver's seat, he kept the door open and leaned in.

"Not a word of this to anyone. Unlock your phone and give it to me."

Again, she did not resist but handed him her cell. He opened the photo app and sent the picture of the skeleton to the trash. Then he wiped it from the trash bin.

"Here you go," he said, handing the iPhone back to her. "This is for your own good, Daisy. I'm not certain of what we're gonna find here, but these are dangerous people behind this. Now go home and forget about it."

"But Nathan…," she began.

"No buts. Don't meddle in this."

With those words he shut the door and walked away. Back to the crime scene.

She was dying to ignore his command and follow him. He had hurt her feelings when he referred to her own investigation as "meddling." Not wanting to be further embarrassed in front of Ben and the deputies whom she had known for years, she started the engine, did a Y turn, and drove to the office.

Lucky he didn't think to check my email.

She parked in the large lot beside the no frills brick building which housed the newspaper. Upon entering she went straight to the editor's office and entered without knocking.

Chad Melbourne scowled. "I heard about what happened."

"I guess Ben told you," Daisy said. "I'm sure he exaggerated. You know how he is. So protective of me. He's been that way since he was my teacher at Franklin High. Protective."

Having run out of ways to discredit Ben Williams' concerns, she stopped talking.

"I know Ben very well. He's not prone to exaggeration. He also asked that we sit on this story until they know more."

She decided not to respond but went on the attack.

"Look! I've got a story for you. Front page. And a photo!"

She located the photo of the skeletal remains in her email and showed it to Chad.

"Damn, Daisy. I'm not going to put that picture in the paper. Where is this?"

Rather than simply answering his question, Daisy elaborated, "Right now Ben Williams and Nathan Stark, the FBI agent, are out at the cabin near the Cullasaja Gorge. This skeleton is in a smokehouse there. They've got cadaver dogs looking for more remains, and they're finding them."

She paused to let that sink in and then continued, "I haven't told Jake that I went there without him, but I'd like to go again with him to take more photos and prepare a video of the scene."

"This is exactly why Ben contacted me. Do you understand what *sitting on a story* means?"

"Yes, sir," Daisy said. She did not add that the only reason she was asking for his approval to go back with Jake was that she hoped to find Keira, still alive, on that remote road.

"Then do it. I just learned that Aldi is planning to come to Franklin. Contact the mayor about that."

Chad fiddled around with papers scattered on his desk and stacked them neatly.

"Will do."

If Daisy felt the need to cross her fingers when she lied, she would have done that now. She had no intention of abandoning her search for Keira. As she left Chad's office, she wondered how she could get Jake to help her.

If he doesn't agree to go with me, I'll have to go on my own. I've got to help Keira, and I know she is near that cabin.

CHAPTER

35

A s she drove toward Jake's work, Daisy saw a band of jet-black clouds crawling over the mountains. Shoving the sunshine out of its way, the clouds colored the mountains, trees and all, with the same black tinge. A prudent person would get off the road and seek shelter. Daisy continued on her way to pick up Jake. She could tell everyone she had not planned to go alone.

Not wanting to give Jake the opportunity to argue with her, she decided it best to text Jake her plan: *on way to pick u up. CM wants video of search at cabin.*

She entered the text but did not look at his reply until she parked in front of Drake Enterprises, where he worked.

Won't go to cabin. Will go to Swan trailer

She knew he was not going to give in, and she had wanted to take another look at the mobile home where she had been attacked.

out front. hurry

Five, ten minutes later. Just as she was about to go without him, Jake walked out. As he climbed into the Jeep, she said, "Where's your gear? We might need to take photos or shoot a video report."

Putting his hand on hers to stop her from shifting gears, he laid down his ground rules for this mission.

"We're just going to have a look. Maybe ask around the trailer park to see if anyone has seen Keira in the last few days. If we find anything unusual, out of place, we're calling Ben's office. Juanita should be able to reach him on their shortwave. Understand?"

Daisy turned away from him but nodded.

"Agreed?"

Daisy was silent and still.

"Daisy, I need to hear you say it."

"Okay, okay, I agree."

Just short of cursing both Chad and Jake for butting in on her plans, she instead cursed herself for involving them in the first place. She would have to make the most of the day.

Turning onto the highway to Atlanta, she thought of ways to get Jake to enter the trailer where she had been assaulted. The best idea she had was to simply walk into the trailer so he would have to follow. To make sure she was safe.

Daisy turned onto the asphalt road that led to the Hillside Mobile Home Park. It was a steep drive, but it was not long until they arrived. She peered down each row of trailers and hoped to see Poppy, the spaniel, and her owner to see if they had any gossip about the trailers. No luck.

When they reached the road at the top of the hill, Daisy turned in and parked across from the first trailers, joined by a splintered walkway, that were home to the Swans. She switched the engine off.

"I was attacked in the one on the left. I think we should go in to see if it's still the same. Given what happened at the cabin I was taken to."

Jake was not going to move so fast. He did not respond to Daisy. Instead, he studied the area uphill from the mobile homes. Tall grass grew from the edge of the road, into a ditch, and then several yards to the edge of a thicket of mountain laurel and rhododendron. Farther off the white oaks took pride of place and soared above the mountain ridge. Nothing was in bloom now, but he said, "It must be beautiful in the spring."

Beauty which Keira must have enjoyed amid the squalor of her family's existence.

He turned to look at the row of trailers and said, "Let's walk down the road a bit. See if anybody's home." With that he opened the door and walked around the Jeep to where Daisy was getting out.

Not to be deterred from her goal of searching both of the Swans' trailers, Daisy said, "Why don't we split up? I can take this half while you check out the others."

When Jake did not reply, she muttered under her breath, "To save time."

"I'm not in a rush, are you? Somewhere you need to get to?"

Jake's eyes twinkled. He knew all of Daisy's tricks.

"Come on. Let's walk to the end and work our way back."

Daisy counted the trailers. Eight. She ambled along to give herself more time to think about how to shake Jake off. No signs of life at any of the homes, but there were cars parked in front of the fourth and seventh. They walked to the end to a trailer that looked well-cared for but had all the blinds closed. An ADT sticker on a window. An ADT sign in the yard.

"I suppose this is a fall or weekend place for a family."

The seventh home had flowers, impatiens, planted at the front. The steps and small landing at the front door needed painting, but it seemed obvious it was occupied. Jake took notice and then continued walking along the road.

"Shouldn't you knock on that door?"

Jake continued to walk silently.

Next home, no car, but the curtains were drawn open and pots of geraniums bloomed cheerfully on the small front porch.

Similarly at the next trailer the blinds were open, and a small patch of tomatoes and marigolds looked to be well-tended.

An old Chevy truck with an extended cab was parked in front of the fourth trailer that appeared to be abandoned.

Daisy began to speak again but did not as Jake was not responding to her.

He stopped at the short pathway to the third mobile home. Deserted-looking, it was shut up tight. Screen door missing. Broken glass on the window next to the door.

Jake put his index finger to his lips and pointed to a well-worn path through the weeds to the Swan family's cinderblock steps. He took Daisy's elbow and guided her across the road to the red Jeep.

As they drove away, he said, "Did you notice the second trailer? A curtain moved. Someone was watching us."

Daisy looked in the rearview mirror as they drove away. No one followed them, and she was still frustrated over not being able to inspect the Swans' trailers on her own.

CHAPTER

36

After dropping Jake off, Daisy decided to go back to the Hillside Mobile Home Park. She wanted to know who had parted the curtain to look at her and Jake, but her plan was thwarted when her cellphone rang.

Chad Melbourne, the *Franklin Free Press* editor, was calling.

"There's been a rockslide on the Sylva road. Get up there as fast as you can. I'll call Jake."

She was almost to the Murphy Highway, so she took the ramp and joined the traffic to Sylva, Waynesville, and Asheville beyond.

No one has heard about the rockslide. I hope they learn about it before going up the mountain.

Hoping to stay ahead of the pack, she floored it and soon began the climb uphill. She looked ahead and saw blue lights at the start of what she knew was a sharp curve in the road. Getting as close as she could, she parked, not bothering to get off the roadway. She grabbed her bag and ran as she looked for anyone she knew without luck until she came upon a Macon County Deputy Sheriff's car.

She walked on and soon enough found Deputy Sheriff Keshawn Hill, Gloria's son.

"What's happened, Keshawn? Chad told me there's been a rockslide. Was anyone hurt?"

The young deputy shook his head. "Lucky that the driver saw what was happening and stopped before he got there. He's in shock, realizing what might've happened. I don't know if it's a rockslide that caused this, but half the highway broke off."

"You're kidding?"

"Not about this." He shook his head vigorously. "This road is going to be closed at least all day today. Then it'll be one lane for months until it can be rebuilt. It's a dang mess. I think the Sheriff is at the bottom of the mountain to block the road and turn traffic around. Someone from Sylva is on the other side doing the same."

Daisy asked, "Can I get a little closer?"

"I dunno, Daisy," he said as he looked around and behind himself. "I reckon you can go for just a little while if you don't tell anyone I let you."

Daisy nodded and moved forward until she reached a barricade. On the right she saw the ragged edge of the asphalt and, when she looked up the hill to her left, she saw a typical Appalachian forest of red and white oak trees and pines with an understory of rhododendron and mountain laurel, no longer in bloom.

This was not a rockslide. When designing the highway,

the engineers chose to go around the mountain rather than tunnel through it. Somehow the supports of the road had been eroded away until it could no longer be effective, and half of the road caved in.

Taking out her iPhone, she shot several photos of the scene. Unsure if Jake would get there in time, she changed the setting to make a video. She emailed those to Chad and began the article.

Early this morning State Highway 441 to Sylva gave way and collapsed. Half of the road is involved. No one was injured in the incident. The road will be closed until further notice. The cause of the cave-in is still unknown. A mixture of soil and clay supported the road so one theory is that the recent heavy rains undermined it. More information will be added as we learn more.

Daisy returned to the Jeep, did minor editing, and emailed the item to Chad. Nothing was happening here, so she decided to find Sheriff Ben Williams. He might know more although she doubted anyone could provide additional information until a civil engineer inspected the area.

She backed up until, arriving at an area with a wider shoulder, she could make a Y-turn to go back toward Franklin. She passed businesses that would certainly be hurting while the road was closed.

Nearing the bottom of the last steep incline, she saw ahead the blue flashing lights of at least two cars. A row of orange barrels blocked the road in front of the vehicles, and a deputy sheriff used a flashlight to wave oncoming traffic to turn left onto Brendle Road and return to town. Ben stood to one side with a group of highway patrol officers. She pulled over to join them.

"Hey, Sheriff Williams." Daisy used a formal address in front of the state officials.

"Daisy," Ben nodded to her. "Come on over. Keshawn radioed that you were just up there."

"Yes, sir. Do you want to see the pictures I took?"

She opened her iPhone and showed the stills and then the brief video.

"Do you have any more information about what happened?"

"No, and I doubt we'll know more until sometime tomorrow. Fortunately, no one was injured, but I can tell you the highway'll be closed for at least one more day."

She looked down the road at the line of traffic detouring to town via Brendle Road. The right lane was clear.

"Can I go straight down the highway?"

"Sure thing."

Daisy took photos of the stream of traffic taking the detour. Then a video which included Ben and the North Carolina Highway Patrolmen. She emailed them to the newspaper, and then she sent everything from the day to Jake. He would be able to weave a coherent video story about the slide, let Daisy do a voiceover, and send it on to WLOS in Asheville.

CHAPTER

37

Storms that had threatened the valley all day reached Franklin. The downpour and low clouds blurred the mountain skyline. No way would Daisy allow herself to get caught in a storm at the trailer park. Instead of going there, she took 441 Business to downtown. If she were lucky, she could catch her dad before he left the office.

She parked in front of Rollie Pollie's and called his office. Mavis answered quickly.

"Dad there?"

"Hey, Daisy. He went to Rollie Pollie's for dinner just before the storm broke. You can probably catch him. I think Ed will pick him up there."

"Thanks, Maxie. I'll drop by later to catch up with you."

She had no umbrella, so she grabbed an old newspaper to cover her head and made a dash for the entrance. She crumpled the now soaking wet newspaper and threw it in the trashcan near the entrance. Joining Lucas at one of the tables, she eyed his French dip sandwich and motioned Beth to bring her the same.

"What brings you to town on such an awful day?" Lucas asked.

"I'm so sick and tired of this rain! When will it stop?"

Lucas chuckled. "The weather doesn't care about your plight. Or maybe the Nunda That Dwells in the Night has got it in for you."

"Really Dad! The Moon God?"

When she was a young girl, either Lucas or her mother would tell her Cherokee myths, including the tale about the sun chasing the moon across the sky. When it rained, they would say the Nunda That Dwells in the Night must be crying.

"Maybe I'll write an article about it. I'm probably not the only person in Franklin who wants to know when the rain will end."

Daisy reached across to snatch a French fry and dip it in the beef bouillon and, although she did not really need to, she said, "I'm starving."

"Good thing your food is here."

Daisy kept her hands in her lap while the plate was set in front of her.

"Thanks, Beth." Before Beth had a chance to leave, Daisy added, "You haven't heard anything from Keira, have you?"

"No," she said. "I heard what happened. About the baby and all. Sure hope she turns up soon."

"We all do. Thanks."

Daisy dunked her sandwich into the broth and took a

mouthful. With her napkin she wiped her mouth where it had dribbled. "Dad...," she began.

"Why don't you swallow that first? You weren't raised in a barn, you know."

They ate in silence for a while and, when Daisy was feeling sated, she started again.

"Dad, I'm so worried about Keira. There are times I'm really afraid she's dead. You heard about the skeleton that was found, didn't you?"

"I did. But that doesn't mean you're going to find Keira there."

"But Dad..."

"Now Daisy, you've always been an optimistic person, a go-getter. Keep working on your story. Let Ben and his crew do the investigating and follow up with him to find out what they learn."

She unwrapped her straw and sipped her fountain Coke. Lucas was right but she could not shake off her bad mood.

Finally, she said, "It's this darn weather."

"Can I join you folks?" Ed said as he sat down. "I snagged a parking place right out front if you're about ready to go."

"Yes, I am," Lucas said. "Do you want to ride with us, Daisy? You could get your Jeep tomorrow."

"No, thanks."

"Suit yourself," Lucas said. Using his cane for support, Lucas led Ed to the door.

Her father was one of the bravest people she knew. He had ups and downs with polio throughout his life, but he never let it get him down.

151

CHAPTER

38

Heavy rain continued to pommel cars creeping along the roads. Fearing a hailstorm might damage her Jeep Sport, Daisy put it in the garage. She stepped into the storm and closed the garage door. She sloshed her way to the stairs that led to her apartment. Soaked to the bone, she did not even bother to step over puddles that threatened to flood the driveway.

Rescue met her at the front door. Tail lifted high and already purring in pleasure but attempting to appear nonchalant, she stretched back first her left leg, then her right. Daisy was not in the mood to coddle the cat. She took off her ruined shoes and soggy socks and dumped them by the door. Going straight to the shower, she let her rain sodden clothes drop to the floor.

As she shampooed her raven dark hair, she thought about the young women whose bodies were being unearthed.

What did they think about when they showered, dressed? Had they gone to high school with her? Church? Did they shop at the same stores? Eat at the same places? Somebody must have missed them. Had everyone just stopped looking? Did they think the women had just run away and didn't want to be found? Why had they been killed and left to rot on that mountain? Why?

Daisy pulled on underpants and an ELO t-shirt, fed Rescue, made a mug of hot chocolate, and got into bed with her journal. How could she make sense of it all?

The promised storm arrived fiercely with more thunder and lightning than previous storms. The thunder rumbled through the valley, and the lightning that followed illuminated Daisy's bedroom. She lay in bed in the dark and counted the time between the thunder and lightning. One Mississippi. Two Mississippi. Three Mississippi. Then One Mississippi. Two Mississippi. The worst of the storm was two miles away, but before she could count again, thunder and lightning clashed over her head.

She got up to look out the window. In the next flash of lightning, she saw large trees inscribing cryptic messages on the sky. Either a tree or a large branch fell on her roof, and a loud crash shook her apartment. The storm hurled itself away. She got back in bed, and the wee calico crawled under the covers and positioned herself by Daisy's knees.

The storm had unsettled her. She turned on the lamp on her nightstand and took up her blue journal. Reading through her recent entries, she thought about Keira. Keira's extended family were petty criminals who dealt mainly in drugs. They also bootlegged liquor and cigarettes to avoid paying stamp taxes on sales.

However, their dealings in the past usually came with spur-of-the-moment violence, for example, when the supplier decided both to take the cash and to take back the goods. Sometimes they would not even bring the contraband and would try to rob the Swans at gunpoint but were forced to flee empty-handed after one of the brothers, most likely George Arthur, Sr., from a sniper's hide farther up the mountain, fired on them. Bodies were either left to rot where they fell or were dragged to be hidden deep in the woods.

Those attacks could not compare to the brutal assaults on ATF agents who discovered their working moonshine still deep in the ivy thickets. The agents would be missed. Unless their disappearance could be explained, federal attention would focus on the valley and ridges until they were found. To avoid further investigation, the agents needed to die in natural accidents.

The Swans, who were generally uneducated, were extremely clever when it came to all manner of murder and mayhem. Once they heard that the Feds were in town, they would get together and hike to their moonshine still.

Most of the time the agents focused on tobacco trafficking as there were few working stills in populated areas. To disable a still, usually two agents would be sent out. The Swans would ambush them and take away their weapons. They would then march them back to their car and push the car off a road with curves and steep drop-offs, and most important, regular traffic so the *accident* would be discovered. One of the Swans would stay behind to dismantle the still and put the components on a sledge to move to another location. Then he would fetch his siblings who were by this time walking back to Franklin.

Daisy returned her attention to the character of the Swan family today. Unlike their ancestors, they were petty criminals who tried to stay off the radar of law enforcement. They also preferred to keep their schemes simple: find and transport drugs, alcohol, and tobacco to other locations in the Smokies. They rarely sold anything in Franklin. Kidnapping did not fit their plans. Too many variables. Police were involved even if families had been warned to leave cops out of it.

Ironically, the Swan family was proud of Keira, even though she shunned the family business. They realized she could be the first in their line to make it to college and a well-paying job. They would never harm Keira.

Daisy was left with a puzzling scenario. She had been attacked at the Swan's trailer, therefore one of the Swans must have attacked her. She tried to think of possibilities but came up short. Everyone knew about their dealing in drugs, cigarettes, and liquor. Kidnapping Keira made no sense because it would have focused attention on those activities and possibly would have shut them down.

If not the Swans, then who?

CHAPTER

39

Winds and rain raged through the night, interrupted frequently by a moaning thunder rolling up the valley ahead of the lightning.

The storms woke Daisy frequently. She got up a few times, went to the bathroom, got a drink of water, and put down fresh water for Rescue who followed her around. Sleep became impossible as her mind raced with thoughts about Keira and what she could do to find her. When the time on her cell phone indicated 5:45, she decided to get up for the day.

Coffee and cheese toast in hand, she sat at the small dining table with a sheet of paper and pen and began to list anyone connected to Keira, excluding Keira's own family for the time being, and anyone whose actions Daisy deemed suspect.

She divided the page into two columns, the one to the

left headed by *Not Likely* and the other *Possible*. She put Lucas, Ed, and Maxie under *Not Likely*, but after considering David Tennant, Maxie's husband, she put him down as a possible suspect. Ben Williams and the deputy sheriffs went in the left column, with a question mark next to Lamar Buxton, who had only moved to Franklin a year ago. Ben took him on because he had been deputized and served for years in Cobb County near Atlanta. Jake and his mother were of course not suspected.

Lexie and Brad? Daisy had known them for years and could not imagine them harming anyone. They went to the column on the left.

David Tennant was the only person so far on the suspect list. She put an asterisk beside his name. She had known Maxie forever and remembered how she could separate the wheat from the chaff, so to speak, and sent most of the Friday night drunk teens home while others she kept in a cell overnight for the sheriff to talk with the next morning.

The teenagers she decided to keep came from homes that provided little guidance. They had fended for themselves for years, taking odd jobs to get money for clothes. They relied on free breakfasts and lunches at school for sustenance. They carried sandwiches and a drink home after school for their dinner. Sometimes they shoplifted clothes or groceries and were arrested and brought to the county jail. Ben had known most of them since they were small children, and Daisy knew he was determined to steer them in a better direction.

Eliminating the Swans from her list of suspects left her totally perplexed.

Who else could there be? Jasmine? Did she want Jasmine to be involved because of jealousy? She was always in Franklin whenever terrible things happened. It wouldn't hurt to put her as a possible. Problem solved.

She had lost her train of thought. Checking her iPhone, she saw it was time to go to work. She got her bag and put the list in.

CHAPTER

40

The trees on the ridgetops trembled in the wind, but the rain had slacked off. Daisy took the opportunity to stop for gas at the BP.

As she was setting up the pump, she saw Jasmine Walker talking with an older woman whose midriff bulge was greatly bulging. When the woman took off in a silver Ford Maverick 150, fully loaded, Atlanta plates, Jasmine got in the passenger side of a yellow Corvette.

Daisy thought about jumping in her car to follow the Corvette. Jasmine's continued presence in Franklin was unusual, and Daisy felt she was not in town to visit her mother. She decided to add Jasmine as a *Possible*, although still wondering if she wanted Jasmine to be implicated because of jealousy. Though in different classes at Franklin High, as cheerleaders they were always being compared. Which had the highest jumps? Who was the cutest? The nicest? Who was the most popular? The friendliest? The smartest? Who had the best boyfriend? Opinions went back and forth between the two girls, but Jasmine usually came out on top.

Daisy pulled into the parking lot beside the nondescript red brick building that housed the paper and went straight to Chad Melbourne's office.

"How's your story on the Sylva highway coming along?"

"There hasn't been anything to add. The weather is slowing the engineers from doing a full evaluation. The road will be closed until next week."

Shuffling her feet, Daisy flipped through her notepad.

"I'm still working on a story about Keira Swan's disappearance. I plan to follow up with the sheriff and the FBI about the bodies found where I was dumped, but I can't imagine that would be connected to Keira. The whole business has me dumbfounded."

"Well, write up the article about the skeleton at the cabin—but keep it low-keyed. I don't want to cause people to panic, to alarm the community with anything sensational when odds are it won't really affect most people," Chad said. "And I really don't want any national news picking up on it. Keep this out of Asheville. Okay? And no pictures."

Daisy nodded in agreement. Any more attention focused on the finding would make her own investigation impossible. As she thought about it, she wondered why she did not panic in situations like this, when an ordinary person would. Had she become hardened to violence and suffering? Was she becoming insensitive? Instead of being afraid and moving fast away from danger, she plunged in, seeking the center, the reason for the danger.

She had not always been this way. Her father and mother raised her to be thoughtful in her approach to life. To care for others. To help others whenever she could. But not by putting herself at risk.

Then her mother died in a single-car accident on a deserted mountain road, and everything changed.

As she reported on crime for the *Franklin Free Press*, she did not shy away from hearing and seeing the nasty details. Whether drug peddling or overdoses, domestic abuse, murder, or rape, she sought details to let the community know to be careful and safe. Her stories were not lurid or sensational but included enough details to illustrate the crimes. She was careful to protect the victims, the innocents.

She was prepared to go wherever her search for Keira took her, and she would not be satisfied until she knew how and why her mother had died.

Chad's voice brought her back to the present.

"Don't forget the city council meeting tonight. They're working on the budget for the coming year, and there are already squabbles on whether a skate park or a dog park is more needed."

Daisy went to her assigned desk and took out her laptop. She uploaded her article about the road leading to Sylva and Asheville along with photos.

She also added the article about the findings at the cabin with photos of law enforcement officials at the scene on the road in front of the cabin. She did not send one of inside the smokehouse with the skeleton of a person, probably a woman. A general description of the discovery of several grave sites in the woods beyond the smokehouse would suffice. She mentioned that the FBI was assisting Sheriff Ben Williams whom she quoted, "We're happy to have the assistance of the FBI with this difficult case. We'll release more details when we have them. I will say now, however, that we do not believe these are the remains of local people."

She added more information about the number of people who vanished from Macon County each year, very few. About old cemeteries which were grown over by nature when the area had been abandoned, many scattered around the county.

Finishing with the admonishment to stay away from the area and that the road had been closed, she did a quick spellcheck and uploaded the story.

She was packing up her things when her cell vibrated. Jake.

"Daisy, want to get together tonight?"

"Sure, I need your help with something. Six-thirty?'

Once she figured out an approach for a detailed story about the *Killer Cabin* as she had come to think of it, she wanted Jake to go along with his cameras and video equipment. She could not publish it now, but Chad might be interested once the crimes had been solved.

If Jake would not help, she would go on her own, and she still needed to revisit the Swans' trailers at Hillside.

CHAPTER

41

Sunlight, which had struggled to find its way through the clouds, finally broke free and the damp green surfaces of the grass and leaves shimmered and dazzled throughout the valley. Daisy hoped it would last until evening when Jake could go back with her to the cabin.

She had only seen Nathan Stark once since the incident last year, and that was when he stood with Ben Williams and others at the smokehouse behind the cabin where she had been taken. As the FBI Special Agent in Charge of the investigation, he could tell her what they had learned about the burials, whether the Swans were implicated in any way, whether they had come upon fresh remains that could be Keira. Whether he *would* tell her was another story.

Sighting a blue Ford Explorer with Atlanta tags, Daisy almost drove by. She had not anticipated that she would be nervous about seeing Nathan again. She shook her head at herself and pulled in alongside it. She assumed he would be in Ben's office and that she could chat with Juanita a bit before meeting him again.

As she walked toward the door, she remembered the day he came to her apartment to check on her. She had discovered Caleb Walker's body, and Nathan had come to her apartment to see if she was all right. She had already met him twice before that occasion and found him attractive.

He had warned her that the FBI believed Caleb to be part of a drug-smuggling ring, to keep what she had seen and knew under her hat. She thought it odd that he came to her place rather than phoning. She had been flattered and was still thinking of him when Jake had shown up.

Where Jake had the sinewy strength that developed through weeks and years of manual labor at the farm, Nathan's build was that of a man dedicated to building and keeping his strength through regular workouts in a gym.

Back then Daisy still thought of Jake as her best friend from high school. She did not see them as a couple and scoffed when others remarked how close they were. She was surprised that, when he later learned about Nathan's visit from Juanita, he reacted jealously.

When she opened the door, the first thing she saw was Nathan sitting in one of the armchairs. She drew back, still holding onto the doorknob, ready to flee, when he looked up with a smile. "Daisy McLaren! I thought I saw you in the crowd at the cabin."

She tried to think of a smart retort like *Nice of you to ask me over*, but she was tongue-tied and simply closed the door.

164

"Is Juanita here?"

Nathan nodded. Daisy walked straight past him and entered Juanita's small office. Juanita glanced up with a puzzled expression and smiled.

"Is Ben here?" Daisy stammered. "I'd like to get more information about the remains found at the cabin."

Juanita smiled knowingly. "Ben is out, but Special Agent Stark should be able to help you."

Nathan Stark took the chair behind Ben's desk and motioned for Daisy to sit in front. "How can I help you, Daisy?"

Daisy fumbled with her notepad and pen. Embarrassed by her own awkwardness, she took a slow, deep breath, adopted a professional demeanor, and began the interview.

"I was actually hoping to meet with you today."

Nathan smiled encouragingly. "Yes?"

"I was knocked out and taken to that cabin. I was left in my own car in front of it."

"I heard. I'm glad you were all right. That must've been a very frightening experience."

Daisy ignored the concern and continued, "I'd been looking for Keira Swan—you've heard about her unusual disappearance?"

He nodded.

"Did you find anyone? Any remains that could have been her?"

To her relief, Nathan shook his head. "No. We found only skeletons and scattered bones. My understanding is that Miss Swan vanished a little over a week ago."

Daisy nodded. "Thank God," she whispered. She

scribbled on her notepad.

"Can you share what you did find?" she asked and quickly added, "I saw the skeleton in the smokehouse."

"We're not ready to release information about everything we found."

"Okay," Daisy jumped in too quickly.

Nathan Stark paused to find the right words. "Why don't you write that skeletal remains were found in the smokehouse? And that they could not be those of Keira Swan as they had been there since before her disappearance? You could end with another appeal for information about Miss Swan."

She had been writing as he spoke and looked up when he stopped. "All right," she said. "Is there anything else I could add?"

"Not at this time, but for your information only, the dogs found seven more sites where victims had been buried. We're still waiting for confirmation, but it seems they must have been concealed around ten years ago at the latest. We expect a forensic anthropologist can be more specific."

"Will you be able to identify them?'

"Susan Parkes is the FA, the forensic anthropologist. She can look for dental records of missing women and check for broken bones and so on."

"So, we'll learn who they were?"

"Maybe, but it's not as easy as TV shows and books make it out to be, especially if the missing women were not reported to anybody, any enforcement agencies. We might not ever know who they all were."

Daisy thought about her mother's missing files on the

girls but decided not to mention them. She did not want Nathan to request them.

"Were there any clues as to who could have done this?"

Nathan shook his head. "Any evidence has been washed away by storms long ago."

Daisy put her note pad away and stood, "If that's all, I'll go."

Nathan also stood.

"I can see myself out," Daisy said.

"I'll let you know when we have more to make public."

She nodded and hurried out, not even stopping to chat with Juanita.

CHAPTER

42

Daisy checked the time on her iPhone. 3:15. She had plenty of time to return home before picking Jake up at Drake Enterprises and was grateful for having those moments to reflect on the discoveries on a deserted road high above the Cullasaja Gorge.

Eight women. Eight girls.

All at once she felt certain that her mother had been trying to learn what had happened to eight young women who went missing while Daisy was away at UNC in Chapel Hill. Alice McLaren was a meticulous woman. In her office as well as in her home everything had a place, and she expected everything to be in its place. She was not a tyrant but had a personality that encouraged acceptance of that rule. Her files could not have simply disappeared.

Either they had been taken from the car when her mother died in what people had assumed to be an accident, or her mother had hidden them somewhere for safety, so they could not be found and destroyed. If she hid them, she must have had a good reason for believing that the information in them would be so damaging to someone that they would risk everything to obtain it. The files would lead to that someone.

Why had her mother not told Lucas where she had put them? Probably because she did not fear for her life. She could not have imagined that anyone, no matter how bad a person they were, would go to that length to protect their identity.

Daisy had long felt her mother's death had not been an accident. Now she had a motive for murder. When Alice McLaren died on that lonely road, the killer must have thought they were safe. Their identity, or clues to their identity, had to be in the missing files. Daisy had to find them.

Where were the places she would *not* have hidden the files? The Department of Social Work for one. There were so many cabinets full of folders related to cases that she could have filed it in the wrong place with a different case name and number which would have made it impossible for anyone to search successfully for it. But Daisy had already gone to her office and believed Gloria had told her truthfully that the files were not there and that she thought Alice McLaren had taken them.

Lucas's office? Again, there were cabinets containing case files from his lengthy law career in Macon County. But no. She would have had to tell him if she hid them there, and she would never put her husband in danger, and for the same reason she would not have hidden them in the house.

If she hid the files anywhere Daisy might be able to find them, only her apartment over the garage remained, but her mother would never have endangered Daisy's life. Perhaps she thought that, since she was away at school, the files would be safe there until she returned after her graduation.

Daisy had reached her apartment. Meowing loudly to be fed and with a quivering tail, Rescue met her at the door. Daisy scooped her up and said, "Are you feeling neglected? Let's feed you now and then I can use your help?"

She poured dry food into one small bowl and filled another with water.

As the calico ate, Daisy looked around the great room. She knew every inch of the room, including kitchen cabinets and drawers. She walked into her bedroom. Again, she could not think of any good place to hide things. Thanks to Rescue's nesting efforts the previous year, she had explored the dark areas of her closet. After Rescue had delivered her litter, Daisy emptied and cleaned the entire closet. No secret hiding places there.

Frustrated, Daisy went to sit on the couch in her living room. Rescue had eaten her meal and was sitting on the floor, legs akimbo, cleaning herself. Daisy flopped her head on the back of the couch and closed her eyes to think. Feeling a soft paw on her nose, she opened her eyes to see the cat staring into her own.

"We aren't quitters, are we, Rescue?"

Suddenly she thought, *the garage*!

Alice McLaren had kept her car there, and after her death, neither Lucas nor Daisy wanted to use it. The only times Daisy parked there were when hailstorms were predicted. Now it occurred to her that her mother had been the only person who regularly went in there. Could she have left the files in the most obvious place for Lucas or Daisy to discover them should anything happen to her? A place used only by herself. She could not have foreseen the future to know how devastated they were when she died.

Daisy had kicked off her shoes and now she put them back on to begin a search of the garage.

Soaking rain had been replaced by a heat wave. The temperature was in the nineties, and the humidity made it feel well over a hundred degrees. Lucas's car was gone. He was most likely at his office, while Ed was using the respite from rain to get groceries without getting drenched in the process.

She raised the garage door and took a moment to do a quick survey. A space for her mother's car took the center. A gas furnace stood in the left back corner. An assortment of garden tools hung from brackets down the left wall. A place for everything and everything in its place.

The brackets closest to the door held a watering can and two aprons with pockets for hand tools. Daisy had loved working in the garden with her mother, side by side, weeding and planning what to plant next. Those were the times her mother had shared her thoughts about life and told Daisy what she thought Daisy needed to know to handle difficult situations that might be strewn on her path.

Entering the garage, Daisy turned to the right wall. At the front, red and green bins contained all the family's Christmas decorations. Her mother had insisted that the items be sorted and stored carefully. Brackets above held both indoor and outdoor extension cords, neatly coiled and ready for the next holiday season. A single orange box held their few Halloween decorations, mainly tools for carving Jack-o-lanterns and lights to make them glow on All Saints' Eve.

Beyond these bins were an assortment of plastic containers and boxes that Daisy had never seen opened. She searched for the light switch and flipped it. The overhead light was very dim. Daisy went to the back of the garage. She groaned at the thought of going through everything but then remembered why she was doing it.

Many of these containers were made of translucent plastic. All were covered with dust and apparently had not been opened for quite a while. Daisy scanned the clear bins and found them to hold things they took to the Outer Banks every summer.

Already perspiring from the heat and humidity, she carried many of the cardboard boxes, legal size, outside to a picnic table where a slight breeze might cool her off. She kept hair bands either on her wrist or in a pocket the whole summer long, so she took a red hair band off her wrist and pulled her dark hair into a high ponytail.

After placing the boxes on the table, she read the labels identifying the contents. Written on many were *McLaren Law* and the dates of files stored up to 1999. Another box was labelled *Family Records*. Daisy took off the top and found a series of files going back to the 1800s when the first McLarens came to the valley, deeds, birth and death certificates, and marriage licenses.

Her heart skipped a beat when she came to a box

marked *Alice McLaren*. She took a deep breath and looked inside. Instead of files she found letters and postcards from the days before she married Lucas. Postcards from her parents and friends who were traveling, letters from her parents and grandparents. Letters from Lucas. The box also held yearbooks from her elementary school through college.

Ready for a second round of boxes, Daisy returned to the garage. The last six were set on an old quilt used to cover more boxes. Daisy moved the boxes and removed the quilt.

Expecting to see cardboard, she was surprised to uncover a cedar chest. It was clearly an antique, simple mahogany with a lock. Its Art Deco appearance suggested it had been bought in the early Twentieth Century. She remembered seeing it at her grandmother's house. For a treat Granny would open it on rainy afternoons and show Daisy her treasures, many of which had been passed down from her mother.

She allowed Daisy to put on the costume jewelry and play dress up with the old clothes. Daisy remembered fondly an enameled case for powder which still had a puff she could use to pretend that she was powdering her nose. When she removed the lid, a spring released a music box scroll playing a few bars of the "Blue Danube Waltz."

There was no key.

Not to be deterred, Daisy shook out the quilt to see if she had overlooked it. She ran her fingers across the beam above the chest and looked for a hook from which a key could be suspended. She pulled it out to look at the sides and back for a hiding place. Nothing.

"Rationally" Daisy said to herself, "the cedar chest stores only Granny's mementos and maybe a few treasures that Mother added."

She pushed the chest back against the wall and covered it with the quilt. She looked through the remaining six cardboard boxes but found nothing. Then she returned all the boxes and bins to their previous spots. She needed to find the key to the cedar chest.

Back in the house she went to the room her parents had shared. Her mother's mahogany dressing table stood near a window that let the natural light in. Daisy pulled out the cushioned bench. As a child, she had sat there many times playing like she was a princess, or Cinderella going to the ball. Her mother never complained when she found her lipstick smushed. She never criticized when her daughter came to dinner with extremely rosy cheeks and red lips. She, Lucas, and Daisy would start dinner like normal until Daisy burst into laughter saying, "Well, do you notice anything different?"

She smiled at the memory and thought how, as an adult, she used little makeup and preferred simple styles. She could not help wondering what she might add to this cedar chest for her daughter, or son, to rummage through someday.

She opened the long drawer first. Most things had been removed but her mother's hairbrush and compact were still there along with earrings in a wooden tray. Daisy removed the tray but found nothing. She felt the back of the drawer. Pulling it out and off its runner, she turned it over and again came up empty.

She repeated the process with all six side drawers and then turned her attention to the tiny drawers attached to the mirror frame. Nothing was in the drawers but, reaching her hand to the back of a slot for a drawer, she felt an envelope.

She could feel the shape of a key and opened the envelope. An old-fashioned brass key with a delicate scroll for the bow, or head. She put the key in a drawer and, after reassembling the vanity, texted Jake, *Plans changed. Need U to move cedar chest 4 me.*

CHAPTER

43

Clouds were gathering above Franklin once more, all in shades of gray and blue. From charcoal to dove gray, tinged with a silver lining. Cobalt and navy blue. Indigo to the blues of faded denim. Light and dark together when the first lightning speared its way from cloud to ground.

Daisy counted Mississippi until she reached seven. She called Jake and was relieved when he answered.

"Where are you? It's going to start raining soon."

"Look out your window, and I'll be there."

She stepped out of the house and sure enough, Jake was pulling into the drive. He went to the back of his truck to retrieve a dolly.

"So where exactly is this cedar chest that needs moving?"

"In the garage."

Daisy worked quietly and quickly to clear the top of the chest. Once she removed the quilt, they pulled it out from the wall. Jake balanced it on the dolly, and they returned to the house.

The first splats of heavy raindrops began to hit the ground, thirsty again after the 90-plus-degree day. "That was cutting it close," Jake said. "Now where do you want this thing?"

"Here." Daisy pointed to a spot on the floor, near the couch but not next to it.

Jake set it down and went to the kitchen to get a beer. "Want one?" Daisy shook her head. She went to her mother's dressing table to retrieve the key.

"Now what's so important about this?"

"I think Mother could've hidden her files in it. The files about missing women," she stopped for a moment, then added, "I think these files got her killed."

Daisy knelt on the area rug and inserted the key. Giving it a twist, she heard the click of the lock. It was open. Daisy looked up at Jake. He raised his eyebrows at her.

"Go on, darlin'. This is what you've been hoping to find."

Daisy threw her head back and let out a big sigh. "What if it's a dead end? Just a chest filled with family memories?'

"Either way, you need to know."

She nodded. Then pushed the top all the way up with one smooth movement.

A tray lying across the top held papers. Letters tinged yellow with age. Various deeds and titles. Passports to cross Cherokee and Choctaw lands.

No files.

Jake lifted the tray and set it on the oak coffee table in front of the couch. Daisy continued to sift through the contents in the cedar chest. Most of the items were those she remembered from her visits with her grandmother. Her own mother had added a photo album of pictures of her, Lucas, and Daisy when Daisy was a baby and then a toddler.

As she removed things, she set them carefully beside her on the floor. Tears filled her eyes when she realized that the only things remaining were just a few old quilts and crocheted blankets. She was just about to return the tray and close the chest when she noticed her own baby blanket, crocheted by her grandmother when Daisy was born.

She wiped her eyes and reached for her pink blanket. As she pulled it up, a thick stack of file folders fell out, bundled together and tied with cord looped across and then up-and-down.

Eight file folders. Eight missing women.

CHAPTER

44

Do you know what this means, Jake? She left them with me, in a place she knew she'd never forget, and that I'd eventually find if anything happened to her.

"She must've agreed with Dad when he said I was just like her."

Daisy held the files close to her chest. She had despaired of ever finding them, of having to give up her quest for the truth about her mother's supposed accident. Now that they were in her arms, she feared learning what they contained, what her mother had found that caused her to be murdered. For now, Daisy had no doubts that Alice McLaren had been murdered. Why else would she have gone to such great lengths to hide them?

Tears trailing down her cheeks, Daisy stood and faced Jake. He encircled her and the files in his arms. Neither spoke.

The soul is in a quiet place. Daisy remembered her mother saying that once. *You have to be still to listen to it.* She had not understood what those words meant.

Daisy had been assaulted at a party in a fraternity house. She had woken up in one of the bedrooms with no memory of how she got there. She had collected her things and crept quietly out of the house. Outside, she had taken out her iPhone and called her mother. Daisy was hysterical. She had no idea of what she should do, where she should go. Her mother could have told her the steps to take. *Go to the UNC hospital and tell them what happened. Then Daisy could tell her story. The hospital will notify the police.* She had waited for her mother to guide her, to tell her exactly what to do.

Alice had no intention of doing that. She and Lucas were raising Daisy to be independent and to value truth, no matter the cost. Her mother helped her gradually calm down, and then said, "The soul is in a quiet place. You have to be still to listen to it."

At that time Daisy had not grasped what she meant. She told no one what happened but kept it hidden inside, locked with other events she chose not to remember. She had planned to discuss what had happened face-to-face with her mother when she returned to Franklin after graduation. She never got the chance.

But now, Daisy understood. Jake allowed her to be in a quiet place. She did not have to carry all the weight alone. She did not have to go through life feeling shame. She trusted Jake to help her, and he always did but not blindly.

She looked up at Jake. He released his hold on her. "Are you all right now?" She nodded, still clutching the files tight in her arms.

"Can we take these up to my place? Before Lucas and Ed get back?"

"Sure thing. Then I'm moving the Jeep into the garage. More bad weather coming."

Daisy could tell by Jake's tone of voice there was no point to arguing.

Rescue chose to ignore them, preferring to jump on the window ledge with a yowl to make it clear that she was snubbing them on purpose. A clash of thunder and lightning made her rethink her plans, and she dashed into the bedroom to sulk.

The forecasted severe weather had arrived. Wind and rain were being pushed rapidly by the force of the storm. The remnants of the tropical storm reached the valley in full force. Daisy rarely used air conditioning during the cooler mountain nights in summer, but now she did. The combination of heat and humidity had caused the air to be stifling.

Jake returned after moving the Jeep.

"I hope we don't lose power," she commented.

It would be a long night.

Daisy placed the files, still bound into a neat package with a piece of string, on the small kitchen table. Now that she had recovered the files, she was reluctant to open them, to read them. She was suddenly anxious about learning what they would reveal about her mother's death.

"Are you hungry?" she asked.

"I'm more curious about the files, but I can always eat something."

Daisy dropped a tablespoon of butter onto the skillet which was quickly heating on the burner. She set out four slices of white bread, smeared them with Duke mayonnaise, put a Kraft Single cheese on two, and, after slapping the pieces together, put them in the sizzling skillet.

"Wish I had a tomato."

With a spatula, she swirled the melted butter to coat the bottom of the skillet and flipped the sandwiches.

She left them alone for a minute. She recalled how her mother had made grilled cheese the same way and wondered if cooking brought her the same comfort it brought Daisy, or if cooking the sandwiches the same way as her mother was what comforted herself.

She pressed hard with the spatula to flatten them, and flipped to the other side, again smashing the sandwiches flat. Another minute and they were done and moved to plates.

Taking a bottle of Coke for herself and a Budweiser for Jake, she set her favorite meal on the table and started eating. Keeping her head down, she avoided Jake's eyes.

"Okay, Daisy. Are we just going to sit here all night?" No reply. "I'm going to look at them if you aren't."

"No!" Daisy covered the stack of files with her hand. "We'll take a look after we're done eating. I need to rest my brain a while."

Jake covered her hand with his own and nodded. "Do you want to go back to the house and wait until Lucas gets home?"

"I don't know."

She did not want her father to relive the loss of his wife.

"Probably not. I want to see what's in them before I tell

Dad."

Hard rain bombarded the structure as if with stones to bring down the walls. Lightning cracked and thunder roared by. Daisy and Jake moved to the couch, with Daisy still clutching her mother's files. Abruptly the storm stopped. Jake said, "It'll probably start up again in a bit. The storm's supposed to last all night."

The silence hung over them like kudzu winding around and threatening to choke out any decision or movement toward opening the files. Jake, usually cautious and slow to act, finally reached for the files out of exasperation. Daisy twisted them away and said, "Okay, okay. I'll look at them."

She laid the bundle on her lap. Daisy noticed that her mother had tied it with a Tiffany bow, her favorite as it is so easy to open. Daisy pulled one piece and then unwound the cord and put it and the folders on the coffee table.

"Do you want me to look at them first?"

Daisy shook her head. "I can do it." She said a silent prayer and picked up the first folder.

The label read Tracy Evans, Maysville, Georgia, 16.

Daisy spread the files to see all the labels: four from North Georgia, three from the area surrounding Franklin, and one from Waynesville.

She was not expecting to get much help from her late mother's office, unless Gloria remembered the young women, so she opened the lone file from Waynesville. Lisa Swanger, Waynesville, NC, 17. Papers inside were held together with a large paper clip. Daisy read the top sheet to herself.

"It's a letter to my mother from the director of the

Haywood County Department of Social Services, Millicent Jordan, dated March 11, 2010. She was starting to look into these disappearances before I left for college."

She skimmed over the rest of the folders. "The last was in February 2015, in Braselton, Georgia. That's near Atlanta."

The other Georgia files contained locations along the I-85 and I-95 corridors.

"I need maps."

"We can get them tomorrow. It's getting late so I'd best get on my way back."

As if on cue, a thrashing of hail pelted the exterior of the apartment to announce the arrival of the rest of the storm.

"I'll get a pillow and covers for you."

CHAPTER

45

Daisy had taken the files to bed. Emotionally drained, she fell asleep with an open folder. Upon waking, she carried it with the others into the great room. Jake was gone, leaving the covers folded with the pillow on top. Rescue was perched on the small ledge of the closed window to watch the rain and wind. The storm was less violent, but the rain showed no signs of letting up.

She Keurig'd a cup of coffee and made cinnamon toast, then sat with her breakfast and the files at the kitchen table. Arranging them in stacks according to state, she took up Lisa Swanger's folder. A record of an interview with Lisa's mother said that Lisa had left early to go to the Mall of Georgia. She wanted to get clothes from A Children's Place for the baby she was expecting in two months. Mrs. Swanger never saw her again.

Another page contained a statement from Lisa's fiancé,

Floyd Smith. They planned to get married before the baby came. They had gone together for a sonogram and learned that it would be a boy. She had asked him to go to Atlanta with her. He regretted that he did not go. He broke down during the interview, and, after checking his alibi for the day, he was ruled out as a suspect. Daisy wondered if he was one of Jake's relatives. She would have to ask him if he had family in Waynesville.

Another note in the file recorded a discussion with a salesperson at A Children's Place who remembered Lisa. She said that Lisa stood out because she was so bubbly. After talking with another expectant mother, who the clerk did not know, the two left the store together.

That was the last sighting of Lisa Swanger. April 12, 2009.

The Gwinnett County Criminal Investigations Division had worked with the Georgia Bureau of Investigation without success. Lisa Swanger's disappearance was classified as an abduction and was filed in the archives as a cold case in January 2010.

The letter from Millicent Jordan was included, and there was a final page, written in Alice McLaren's handwriting, summarizing the inquiry.

Daisy sorted out the three folders from vicinities near Franklin. She recognized one name: *Ruby Frazier.*

Daisy had gone with her mother to visit Ruby's home near Burningtown.

There was a note in her mother's handwriting: *Ruby vanished when her delivery time was one month away. She was in*

*the care of foster parents who reported that she had never been a
problem. She was not the type to run away.*

That disappearance was the spark that set off her
investigation into missing women.

Alice McLaren kept the search a secret from her
Franklin office colleagues and cautioned the social workers
she contacted in Asheville, Atlanta, and North Georgia to
also work under the radar, as she was not sure how or
where the kidnappers found the women.

Daisy read through the rest of the files. The women had
two other things in common besides being missing: they
were all young, 17 or younger. They were all pregnant, just
like Keira. Except Keira had returned to Franklin with a
baby who Daisy now believed to be Keira's own. The others
had vanished without a trace—unless the remains found at
the cabin could be matched with any, or all, of them.

Alice McLaren had uncovered the link between these
missing girls, and that discovery had led to her death. Daisy
was sure of it. Her mother never gave up. She was like the
proverbial dog with a bone. Whoever lured her to her death
must have offered information too good to pass up. If only
Daisy knew who had made that call. No matter. She had her
mother's files and now she would not give up before she
knew who caused the young women to vanish, likely the
same person who had killed Alice McLaren.

CHAPTER

46

Daisy just knew life would be easier if it would just quit raining all the time. She had tired of 100% humidity that was causing damp clothes, soggy shoes, limp hair. She blamed the current weather patterns, as she blamed many things, on global warming, climate change, and rising sea levels. Even Rescue seemed grumpy. She was off her feed, choosing to either sit on her favorite window ledge to watch for birds or to curl up on Daisy's pillow to sleep.

Note to self: *tackle global warming once I find Keira.*

Daisy was stymied. Having decided that the Swans could not be involved in Keira's disappearance, she did not know where to look, which way to turn. She made another cup of coffee and turned the television on to the Weather Channel only to hear that the storms would continue for three more days, but after that the sun would return with a chance of afternoon thunderstorms, the usual weather pattern expected for July.

Determined to spend as little time as necessary outdoors, she decided to visit Retta and Louisa to see how they were getting on. She showered and dressed quickly. Rescue still ignored her. Nonetheless, she commanded her to *Guard the house*!

Traffic was slow-going on the highway, and Daisy kept to the right in the slower lane. Rainwater mixed with road grit was flung onto her windshield by cars rushing by. She passed one fender bender and put even more distance between her and the car ahead.

She thought about driving up the road where her mother had died. Instead, she drove to the next exit for Ruby Mine Road, where Retta's cabin sat at the top of the ridge.

She drove past the mine office and then by the site of the plane crash that led to last fall's investigation of drug smuggling. An investigation that almost got Jake, and her, killed. She hoped she had grown a little wiser and a little less impulsive since. Still, she kept her handgun in the Jeep's glove compartment, just in case she ran into trouble.

As she approached the cabin, she saw the yellow Corvette. Would she find out who had been driving it earlier? Sitting in the Jeep, she reflected on her lingering suspicions about Jasmine. Why had Christian, the drug smuggler, called Jasmine *patron* when she arrived at the Ruby Mine office and shot and killed him?

Daisy did not exactly have a rivalry with Jasmine Walker. They had both been cheerleaders at Franklin High.

Jasmine was a senior when Daisy was a sophomore, and Jasmine had always encouraged her. Now that they were adults, Jasmine always seemed to be watching her warily as if to catch her at something, looking at Daisy aslant, hoping to catch her in an unguarded moment. Daisy realized that, for whatever reason, Jasmine made her feel uncomfortable.

Over the past year Daisy had come to rely on Retta as a mother figure. She had the same relationship with Jake's mother, Clemmie Smith. On the other hand, Louisa Simpson was more like the aunt you loved but were always slightly embarrassed to introduce to your friends as she was likely to blurt out a taboo subject at the worst time.

Daisy opened the door and her umbrella and made a dash from the Jeep to the front porch, the porch on which Retta's husband had threatened her with a shotgun the previous year. She shook out her umbrella and set it by the door.

Before she could reach for the doorknob, the door burst open, and Louisa pulled her into the living room.

"Lord have mercy! Look what the cat drug in, Retta."

She ushered Daisy into the kitchen where Retta, Jasmine, and much to Daisy's surprise, Brad, were having coffee together.

"Louisa, let go of the poor woman! Daisy, sit right down." Retta continued. "Want some coffee?"

Daisy shook her head.

"I should've called. I didn't think you might already have company."

Daisy stuttered.

"Of course, Jasmine isn't company. Are you in town for a while, Jasmine?"

"She's just passing through, like always."

Louisa did not give her a chance to reply but carried on, "We try to get her to stay, but..."

"In fact, I need to get Brad back to town and head to Atlanta."

Jasmine hugged Louisa and her mother.

"Nice seeing you, Daisy."

Louisa busied herself bustling them out the front door.

"Never a dull moment," Retta laughed. "I'm glad you're here. I've had you on my mind lately. I saw your stories about the bodies and the landslide on the road to Sylva. And, of course, I saw the notice about Keira Swan gone missing. Is there any word on her?"

Daisy joined her at the table.

"Afraid not." She paused for a moment. "I found some of my mother's old files, and I think they are about the women whose remains were found. Jake knows, but I haven't told anyone else. Please don't..."

"I won't tell Louisa, or anyone else. No telling how far Louisa's grapevine reaches. Speak of the devil."

Louisa came back into the room talking.

"That Brad is a peculiar fellow. Odd. He's a little old for Jasmine to be hanging around with."

She sat at the table with them.

"Don't you think? And isn't he married?"

Daisy was having the same thoughts, but she chose to keep them to herself. She realized that she did not actually know a whole lot about him. What she did know had been shared by Lexie, after she and Daisy had become close friends. In fact, Daisy counted her as one of her best friends, the other being Jake.

She recalled that Lexie met him while on Active Duty in Heidelberg, Germany. At that time, he was with Military Intelligence.

Lexie and Brad were complete opposites. Where Lexie was quick and fit, Brad was soft and slow. Lexie was dark and sported short dreadlocks. Brad's pale skin burned after less than a morning in the sun. Lexie enlisted in the United States Army after high school. The CIA recruited Brad when he graduated with a degree in Russian.

A shared love of reading brought them together. They had seen each other many times in the base bookstore, and Brad invited her to join him for coffee. He moved in on her quickly and, before Lexie knew it, they were living together.

When they moved to Franklin, Lexie's hometown, they pooled their money to open a bookstore. They purchased Books Unlimited and remodeled it to include a coffee shop. Keira Swan had worked at the coffee bar alongside Joe Taylor, who had died from a heroin overdose last year.

She had already wondered what Jasmine and Brad were discussing when she had seen them together at the bookstore. Maybe Lexie could enlighten her. Maybe there was a simple and innocent explanation.

"That was a nice car out front. Is it Jasmine's?"

"Belongs to one of her Atlanta friends who lent her it," Louisa blurted.

"I'm afraid I have to get back to work," Daisy said and quickly left.

CHAPTER

47

Darn that Louisa!"

Daisy inched along with the rest of the hypercautious motorists enroute to Franklin. She suspected they would stop in Franklin, as no sensible person would plan to drive through the Smokies in this weather. Occasionally, a maniac sped past with car tires spitting water to mix with the sharp pellets of rain attacking her windshield and momentarily blinding her. Blinded by water—who knew?

She cursed Louisa again, rather than the driver or the storm. If Louisa had stopped meddling with everyone, Daisy could have somehow finessed her way into finding out why Jasmine and Brad were so cozy these days. If they were having an affair, she would kill Brad first, then Jasmine.

There were a few problems with that hypothesis. Brad

did not fit the image she had of Jasmine's type. In high school she had always dated ruggedly handsome guys, football heroes, and Brad was a middle-aged, graying, married bookseller. He had worked for an unnamed clandestine intelligence group years ago, but, if he had ever been a buff action spy, those days were long gone. The Brad whom Daisy knew, or thought she knew, was an unobtrusive person. He had gone soft.

Also, he was married. To Lexie, Daisy's best friend. When she compared Lexie and Jasmine, Lexie was the clear winner. Lexie was open, clever, loving, while these days Jasmine, although still physically attractive, came across as a dark, furtive creature.

Daisy pulled in behind Lucas's car and hurried up the ramp and through the back entrance to his office. His door was closed. She heard voices, so she walked on to see Maxie.

"Did Jake leave a map for me?"

"Good morning to you, too," Maxie said without looking up from her typing.

"Sorry, Maxie. It's just been that kind of morning."

Daisy leaned over to hug Maxie's neck.

"You're forgiven," Maxie said as she handed over a 9x12 manila envelope.

"He told me not to give it to you unless you promised not to go anywhere without him."

Daisy laughed as she took out two maps. One showed Franklin north to Waynesville and I-40. The other, Franklin south to the Atlanta suburbs.

"Seriously, Daisy."

Maxie swung her chair around to face Daisy.

"You'd best listen to Jake this time."

"But..."

"No but's!" Maxie stopped her from arguing. "I shouldn't tell you this, but I overheard Lucas talking with Ben. Agents from the DEA are also meeting with Ben and Nathan. Looks like they're planning to do something big."

"What could the Drug Enforcement Agency have to do with Keira's disappearance?"

"I don't know that it does," Maxie said, "but you can be sure that where drugs are involved, the Swans are not far behind."

"Do you think Dad would..."

"No, and before you ask, he's going to be tied up later this morning trying to mediate a divorce."

"Okay. I give up," Daisy said, "but let me ask about something completely different."

"Shoot."

"I was just up at Retta's cabin, and her daughter Jasmine was there with Brad. It's the second time I've seen them together. The first was at the bookstore, and they seemed to be arguing. Do you know any reason they'd be together?"

"Wow, no! Have you asked Lexie? Or Brad?"

"I don't want to talk with Lexie about it until I know what's going on, and I think Brad would lie to me."

Maxie cupped her chin while putting her fingers across her mouth, then she said, "You know Brad was working for a while in North Atlanta. Perhaps they met there."

"I'm really wondering why Jasmine would be involved with Brad. You don't think they're having an affair? Do you?"

"I don't know. Ask her mom. Ask Retta."

"If I can get past Louisa. Maybe I'll call her. But what am I thinking! I can't ask her if her daughter and Brad were having an affair."

"I meant to ask if they met in Atlanta."

Daisy turned to leave but stopped and looked back at Maxie.

"I found my mother's files. The ones that she had with her just before she died. There were eight files about young women who went missing. They were all pregnant."

"You think those are the bodies that were found?"

Daisy nodded.

"I'm going to take them to Ben so he can make copies of them. You know, for the first time I'm feeling that I can't do this anymore."

"Do you mean looking for Keira?"

"Everything. It seems like I just keep learning more horrible things about Franklin. I'd like for things to go back the way they used to be."

"You can't change the past, but you can, the future," Maxie got up and hugged Daisy. "Ali would be so proud of you. I know Lucas is. You're so much like your mother."

Daisy wished she could explain how the more she learned about her mother's last days, the more sorrowful she became. Heartache could not explain the weight that hung where her heart should be. She shrugged off the memory even though she knew grief was only a heartbeat away.

CHAPTER

48

Daisy went straight to the sheriff's office and left her mother's files with Juanita Williams. She said she would come back in an hour or so to collect the originals. They were precious to her since they were so important to her mother. The contents provided clues to why her mother died. Daisy was certain now that Alice McLaren had been murdered, that the accident was used to cover up crimes, but the files shed no light on who had done it.

Who was so threatened by her mother that they needed to kill her?

Still wondering about Brad and Jasmine, she decided to go by the bookstore to see Lexie. To see how Lexie was doing. Whether or not she was upset. Was it possible Brad was leaving her for Jasmine?

Lexie was behind the counter facing a line of customers. Brad was nowhere to be seen.

"Can I help?" Daisy asked as she was already walking behind the counter.

"Please! Can you bag the books as I ring them up?"

The two women worked quietly and efficiently and were soon caught up for the moment. Even as they caught their breath, more customers sauntered in, leaving their soggy umbrellas by the door.

"Do you want me to open the coffee bar?" Daisy said.

"That would be fantastic. On days like this we can make as much money on coffee as we do on books. I still haven't found a good replacement for Keira."

Rainy days brought disgruntled gem seekers to stores in search of other ways to fill the time until the sun came out and they could go back to sifting through dirt for jewels. They had several choices: the bookstore, Ruby City Gems (to buy stones they were not able to find), antique stores, and art stores. Many gemstone tourists were so vexed that they packed up their campers or checked out of the hotels and returned either to their homes or to the next stop on their vacations.

"I'm so glad you're here. Bring us coffee, why don't you?"

"Where's Brad?" Daisy asked innocently when she returned with two mugs of coffee, one marked *His* and one *Hers*.

"He called and said he had an errand to run. Not sure what. I guess I'll find out if he ever gets here. That was hours ago."

Daisy was in a quandary. It was a perfect time to tell Lexie what she had seen. To have been so eager a few minutes ago, the customers were taking their time to browse among the stacks of books. She just could not bring herself to discuss Brad. Not yet. Daisy procrastinated. She set her mug on the counter and opened a UPS box containing remainders—first editions of a mystery that had not sold very well.

"What should I do with these?" She read the title aloud. "*Cul-de-sac Murders*. Could've used a better title."

"Put it in the back room with open box sales. Fifty cents apiece."

Glad for more time to consider how to ask her about Jasmine and Brad, she carried the box back. When she returned, she was shocked to see Brad also behind the counter.

"Daisy! Twice in one day."

He hugged Lexie.

"I just ran into her up at Retta's place."

"Oh?" Lexie said absent-mindedly.

"Yeah. I'd run up there to see how she and Louisa were getting along."

He winked at Daisy.

Now Daisy was even more confused. No mention of Jasmine and after the way he explained his presence at the cabin, it would be only natural that she would be visiting her mother. Daisy grabbed a stack of paperbacks, mysteries by John Hart.

"Where can these go?"

"John Hart. He's an excellent Southern writer. Put them on the 'Recommended' rack up front."

Having decided that she did not want to discuss Brad, her mother's recovered files, or the bodies, for she had come to think of the remains as bodies with names, she felt she would not accomplish anything with Lexie today.

"Will do. Then I'm off."

It was time to go to Waynesville.

CHAPTER

49

Before going to Waynesville, Daisy went to retrieve the originals of her mother's files. Juanita Williams was alone in the office. The eight files were stacked neatly on her desk.

"Before you ask, I have no idea where they went," she told Daisy. "They're being even more close-lipped than usual."

She handed Daisy the files.

"Can you let me know when you find out?"

"I will, but I think I might be the last to know."

Daisy considered driving back to the cabin where the remains were found but, figuring that getting there would take too much time and that realistically they could be anywhere, she decided to continue to Waynesville. The trip there would take an hour or more in the heavy rains, and the one lane traffic where the road had caved in would add extra time.

Back in her Jeep, she called the DSS there to confirm that Millicent Jordan was at work.

The Department of Social Services was in the same complex as the Haywood County Sheriff's Office. Like newer public buildings in the mountains, it was a bland, red-brick structure. When Daisy pulled into a parking space, her hands began to tremble.

"Now was not the time to panic," she told herself as she began to breathe slowly and deeply. "She probably won't tell me anything I don't already know."

Folders in hand, Daisy entered and announced herself at the reception desk.

"Of course. Millicent told me you were coming. She had to go out, but she told me to take you into her office to wait. Would you like a Coke or coffee?"

Daisy followed her.

"No thank you."

Left alone, she untied the cord used to keep the folders together. She took out Lisa Swanger's file. Lisa had seemed the odd girl out until Daisy discovered that she had left home to meet friends at the Mall of Georgia. That tied in with the other disappearances that happened between Franklin and the area north of Atlanta.

She planned to ask Millicent Jordan about her last conversation with Alice McLaren. Then she would tell her about the discoveries at the cabin and her suspicions that the remains were those of the eight missing young women in her mother's files. She did not have to wait long before Millicent, taking off her raincoat to hang on a coat tree, entered the office.

"It's so nice to finally meet you, Daisy. Your mom told me so much about you. She was enormously proud of you."

She was younger than Daisy had been expecting. A tall, thin woman with a neat Afro. She must have been just beginning her career when Alice McLaren contacted her.

Daisy had stood when Millicent entered, and now they both sat.

"What happened to those girls was such a tragedy! It still shocks me to think about it—even with all I've seen and heard over the years."

"That's why I'm here. In a note I found in the folder, she mentioned a phone call with you, but she didn't say what it was about."

Millicent nodded as she took up her copy of the file that was centered on her desk.

"That's right. I was surprised she never got back to me about Lisa, but I suppose she's been too busy."

Daisy gasped, "You haven't heard?"

She searched for the gentlest way to say it and decided, as is often the case, that the easiest way is also the best. "Mom is dead."

"No! I'm so sorry. I hadn't heard. When did she pass on?"

"That's why I'm here today. The note."

Daisy looked down on the folder she held in her lap.

"I think you were the last person to talk with Mom."

Tears welled up in Millicent's eyes.

"I'm so sorry for your loss."

Shaking her head to ward off the tears, Millicent opened the folder in front of her and looked through the reports. She removed one from the ob/gyn she sent Lisa to, along with her latest ultrasound.

"Lisa was 26 weeks (about 6 months) pregnant. The ultrasound shows a healthy baby boy."

She handed the ultrasound to Daisy.

"I remember how excited she was. She said Floyd, Floyd Smith, was going to be so proud and that they would soon be married. Married before the baby arrived. They planned to name him Floyd, Jr. She asked me if I would come to the wedding, and I said of course."

Millicent began to sniffle and took a Kleenex from the box on her desk.

"I never got an invitation. After Ali told me that several girls, all about to have babies, had gone missing around Franklin and that she suspected Lisa might be among them, I assumed that's what had happened. But that was what, almost ten years ago. Why are you asking about Lisa now?"

"Like I told you, you were the last person my mother spoke to about the young women. Later that week, she got a call and must've gone to meet someone about them. We were told she had an accident on a road on the mountains outside of Franklin and had died.

"I never believed that it was an accident. Mom was a careful driver and was used to the worst kinds of mountain roads."

She looked up, as if to heaven, and then directly into Millicent's eyes.

"The skeletal remains of eight women have just been discovered behind a cabin above the Cullasaja Gorge. I think Mom was killed to hide the truth about what happened to them."

"That's terrible, if true," Millicent said.

"I believe that whoever killed her was after her files, but she hadn't taken them with her. She'd removed them from her office and hidden them. I only found them this week."

"I should've followed up with your mother," Millicent said, "but I was so new at the job. Felt overwhelmed with everything, to tell you the truth."

Daisy explained how she had become involved when Keira Swan had vanished leaving an infant behind with friends. How Daisy searched for her at the Swan's trailer, had been knocked unconscious and woke up in her own car at the cabin where the remains were discovered. It was not far, as a crow flies, from the road where her mother had died.

"When I learned her files were not at the Department of Social Services, I began to look for them. It wasn't easy but I finally found them in my grandmother's cedar chest that was extremely well-hidden in our garage."

Holding Lisa's file close, she sighed.

"There are eight folders. I think they'll help identify the eight bodies at the cabin."

Daisy had hoped that Millicent Jordan would give her information that could help explain Keira's strange disappearance. About to leave, she remembered the primary reason for her visit.

"You were the last person to speak with Mom. Did she say anything else?"

"She hoped to find out what had happened to the girls. Your mother said she was going to meet someone. That she had told Ali she knew what had happened and who had taken them."

"She?" Daisy asked. "Mom was meeting a woman. Did she say who she was?"

Millicent shook her head.

"I don't think she knew, but now I wish I'd thought to ask."

CHAPTER

50

For Daisy to say that she was relieved when she finally made it home was an understatement. Physically and emotionally depleted, she sat for a few moments with her head resting on her hands which still gripped the steering wheel.

Jake's Dodge Ram was parked in the driveway. Lights were on at Lucas's and in her apartment. She simply wanted to be alone. To collapse on her bed. To sleep without dreams.

The storm was dumping more rain than usual. She jumped out of the Jeep without taking the files and rushed up the stairs. At the top the door stood open, and Jake waited. As he caught her in his arms, she realized that was exactly what she needed tonight—to be cared for. The day had left her feeling vulnerable. Insistence on her independence had sent her adrift without anchor or mooring. In Jake she had found an anchor. With Jake she could give in to her doubts and worries.

Neither spoke. Jake led her to her shower. He turned on the water and left for a moment to get fresh towels. When he returned, she was still just standing there, at a loss of what to do with herself. He helped her undress and step into the shower. Then he left her alone.

Rescue purred on Daisy's pillow beside Jake. When Daisy turned off the shower, she dashed to greet Daisy who emerged with her body and hair wrapped in towels. She stooped to scratch the tiny calico between her ears. A t-shirt and panties were folded at the foot of the bed. She put them on, and silently crawled under the covers.

He got up to leave, but she took his arm.

"Please don't leave me alone."

He lay down next to her and encircled her with his arms.

Daisy and Jake were swimming in the Little Tennessee just below the Macon County Library. They accessed it from a hiking trail that looped around to start and end at the library.

When younger and meeting friends there, they would often go skinny-dipping. When Daisy returned from UNC for the summer, they wore swimsuits, or, if they had not planned to swim, underwear. They splashed each other playfully with the warm water and failed to notice that a current, growing stronger and stronger, had carried them to the top of the waterfall at the Cullasaja Gorge. The thunderous roar of the cataract resolved into a tumultuous crash on the boulders below.

As their bodies joined with the treacherous waterfall, Daisy cried out, "It's in the wrong place."

She woke from the nightmare abruptly to Jake's shaking her by the shoulders.

"We've got to go. Chad just called. There's been a mudslide west of town."

Confused, Daisy stared at him until she realized what he had said. "Where? Is your farm okay? Lexie and Brad's?"

"Past there. Chad said he thought it was out the Arrowwood Branch."

"Arrowwood?"

"You know, Arrowwood Creek. Get a move on it."

CHAPTER

51

What did Chad say? Exactly."

"Not much," Jake said. "To get out there asap. He's getting lots of calls. The main one from the LBJ Job Corps folks, saying they'd heard a roaring sound from up the mountain."

Jake slowed to take the turn to connect with Wayah Road. Before they could turn at Loafer's Glory, they heard blasts of the siren and horn signaling a fast-approaching fire engine. Its lights flashed as it slowed to make a sharp right turn.

Daisy and Jake pulled into the lot at Loafer's Glory to wait until they could be sure that no more emergency vehicles were coming.

"It's stopped raining," Daisy said. The rain had not completely ended but had slowed, and she caught glimpses of Carolina blue sky peering over the mountains. She could catch glimpses of gaps, that allowed roads to be built, zigzagging through the ridges.

"That should be long enough."

Jake eased out of the parking lot.

Daisy could not remember the last time she went to the Job Corps facilities on Wayah Road. In high school, she volunteered to tutor teens in reading and math. She recalled that Arrowwood Road was directly across from the center, which was only a couple of miles from Loafer's Glory.

Just as Jake signaled a right turn and slowed down, they heard an explosion.

"Hurry," Daisy said.

She punched the quick dial for Chad.

"We're on Arrowwood and just heard an explosion. I'll let you know what it was when we reach the site. Better tell the public to keep clear of the area."

She dug around in her bag for pen and paper, then began to describe what was happening.

Arrowwood was another neglected dirt and gravel road that followed the creek part of the way uphill. They had passed several houses and trailers when suddenly the road veered sharply away from the creek.

There had not been enough time for the area to be cordoned off with yellow and black crime scene tape. Indeed, no law enforcement had arrived yet. The volunteer firefighters had parked their engines and a water tender far back from the trailer and were watching, letting the fire, which had resulted from the explosion, burn itself out.

Daisy had covered enough similar explosions to know that the trailer had probably housed a methamphetamine lab, where crystal meth was produced. Ordinary household bleach was favored in the area as the spark to create a chemical reaction with pseudoephedrine to make the meth.

Bleach was readily available and could be purchased without creating suspicion. The sale of nasal decongestants that contained pseudoephedrine had been severely restricted after the passage of the Combat Methamphetamine Epidemic Act in 2005. Pseudoephedrine could no longer be sold in amounts needed for large-scale production. It was only available with a prescription. It had to be smuggled into the mountains, and an area such as the Smoky Mountains, already having a history with moonshine stills and bootlegged alcohol, was ready-made for the smugglers to enter and encourage the conversion of homes into meth labs.

The windows on an old Mustang, parked near the trailer, were shattered in the blast.

"Was anyone inside when it blew up?"

She had gradually moved closer to the captain of the volunteer fire department.

"Do you know who the car belongs to?"

"Don't know about the car, but someone must have been inside to set this off," he said. "I imagine they were trying to get rid of it before we got here. They were probably here when the mudslide happened and figured that we'd be on the way."

Ben Williams pulled up and directed deputies to set up the boundaries of the restricted area. Nathan Stark soon followed. Daisy looked around for Jake and found him busily recording a video of all the activity. Joining him, she said, "What do you think? The Swans?"

"Probably. I think they've got some kin living in one of the houses we passed on the way up here. Maybe cousins."

Daisy scanned the woods surrounding the trailer and said, "I don't see any signs of a mudslide. Are you sure it was around here?"

"Yeah. Someone called it in from the Job Corps. I guess you had to be back from the road to see it."

Now Jake was taking still shots of the scene.

"Are you ready to send photos to Chad? I'm about to text my copy."

"In a minute."

Daisy saw that, beyond the crowd and fire engine blocking the way, the road continued up the mountainside. After sending her report to the paper, she cautiously walked around the scene and slowly climbed the slope.

Whatever gravel had once tried to hold the dirt in place had disappeared long ago, and deep grooves serpentined through the remaining ground.

She reached the place where the road again followed along Arrowwood Branch. The branch, a tributary of Wayah Creek, was swollen and fast flowing after the recent heavy rains. It soon left the roadside, and Daisy also left to walk beside it. She glanced back to see if anyone had noticed her.

"I probably should've told someone where I'm going," she said to herself, realizing that an unleashed potential for damage remained in the current as it rushed downhill. She reached out her hand to support herself on a granite boulder as she climbed. The torrent twisted to the other side of the boulder.

This uphill trek seemed to take forever when a single-lane, red-clay road emerged from the oak forest at a low bridge to cross the Arrowwood. She could see that the road turned to the left on the other side to go farther up the mountain.

Daisy stood for a moment trying to decide whether she should attempt to cross the bridge but decided against it. The cascade was slowing. As the waters receded from the banks, they left a red sludge in their wake. As granite was eroded over the millennia, kaolin was formed, and, of the remaining minerals, it was iron that gave this clay its famous red color.

Though it seemed to take forever, she soon reached the spot where the mudslide had stopped. Whole trees and broken limbs formed a dam that collected junked cars, old tires, broken furniture, bits and pieces of cabins, and the decaying body of a woman whose age could not be determined.

It was clear to Daisy the person died before the mudslide carried her away. She could see where her abdomen had been slashed and left gaping. She was relieved to see that it was not Keira's body. She took out her phone and called Ben, not Jake, to report what she had found.

"You better get up here. I've found another body," she said. "I'm climbing up by the creek and can meet you at the top of the mudslide."

CHAPTER

52

Green tendrils of kudzu creeping close to the creek's edge was the first sign that Daisy was nearing a homestead. The oaks that rose above young trees, white pine or black cherry, created shrouds of broad green leaves. Wishing she had brought a snack and water, she sat on a flat boulder to rest before making a final effort to reach what she hoped would be a cabin and Arrowwood Road.

The kudzu line stopped at a gravel lot beside a log cabin but still covered a split-rail fence Daisy had to climb over. The Sheriff's car and several others were parked in the lot. She groaned as she recognized Jake's truck. She could feel another lecture coming on. Lowering her head, she crossed to the cabin and, nodding to Keshawn who was posted at the door, entered.

"I'm gonna have to ask you to leave, Daisy."

Only two people were in the cabin, Ben Williams and a

woman who Daisy believed to be a forensic specialist. Both were clad in white plastic suits, blue shoe covers, and gloves. Both were wearing N95 masks that had become so prevalent during the COVID pandemic.

Scanning the room as she backed out, she saw a bed, a refrigerator, and a door to the right where a wall had been constructed to divide the room in two. At the last second, she saw a crib.

Exhausted from her climb and depressed at the thought that Keira might be one of the women who had been kept here, she sat on one of the rocking chairs on the porch. People wearing vests or jackets indicating their agency or department were combing the area for evidence.

Jake came from the back of the cabin.

"Take a look at these."

He pulled the other chair close to Daisy and sat. He gave a running commentary as she scrolled through the photos on the digital camera's small screen -- barrels used to burn trash, plastic bins with lids (a slot had been created in the top to insert objects that wouldn't burn like needles and scalpels), and the contents of that bin.

He closed the screen and said, "There were even plastic bags full of women's clothes and shoes. They're going through that now."

"Keira?" Daisy asked.

"They won't know until they've sorted through it all."

"More bodies?"

Jake gritted his teeth.

"Yes. Now let's go. We're not going to get more info until later."

Daisy wanted to forestall another lecture and

considered walking back to her Jeep but, remembering she still lacked water or food, she got in his truck. Jake turned the key, shifted into reverse, and stopped.

"Daisy, I want you to stop this right now. Has it occurred to you that you could be putting Keira's life in danger?"

She drew back and scowled.

"What do you mean?"

Jake backed onto the road, shifted into first, and stopped again.

"Do you think you're the only person hunting for Keira? Isn't it possible that someone else might want to stop her from saying where she's been? What she knows?"

Daisy said nothing. She knew he was right but bristled at the thought of having to give up her search.

"There's a chance I could find her first. And help her."

"You're unbelievable," Jake said as he started to drive down the road.

"Just drop me off at my car."

Neither spoke again. He stopped to let her get out, and they went their separate ways.

CHAPTER

53

Daisy slept in the next morning. Rescue was already on her perch when she entered the great room. She pawed at the window until Daisy opened it to give the cat more room. Rescue pricked her ears up and swung her head back and forth as she spotted a Carolina wren flitting about. She chittered at the thought of capturing the bird. Daisy absentmindedly scratched the cat between her ears and went to make coffee.

The memory of Jake's admonition, or lecture as she always tagged his advice, still upset her. Usually writing about problems in her journal lessened their impact on her tranquility. *A problem shared is a problem halved.* Advice from her mother. Since her mother's death, she had not been able to trust others with her true problems, not even Lucas or Jake. She now regarded writing in her journal as sharing. Indeed, she had only begun to keep a journal when her psychologist, Dr. Ammons, recommended it after her mother died.

Increasingly she turned to Jake with thoughts and impressions. What he said yesterday caused her to question her trust in him. He had driven her to her car and left. She had not asked, and he had not come over later. She regretted it now.

Exhausted by her hike to the abandoned cabin and distressed by not finding Keira, she had needed to be held and comforted. Jake seemed intent on making her reflect on her actions and the results of those actions. Self-reflection. Not a ready part of her tool kit. As a journalist, she turned her focus outward. She was a fact gatherer. She repeated facts in her articles without giving any judgment. That, she left for Chad Melbourne, the editor of the *Franklin Free Press*.

She thought of calling Jake but decided against it. She needed to get to work.

The Sheriff's office was quieter than she had expected. His wife, Juanita, was sorting papers at her desk. Seeing Daisy, she said, "I heard about yesterday. When's it gonna end?"

"When the Swans are arrested and tell us what has happened to Keira," Daisy said, although she feared having that knowledge.

Previously she had discounted their involvement, but with the discovery of the meth lab, they again became suspects. Where there were drugs in Macon County, a Swan was likely to be close by.

"We might learn it sooner than you think. Ben and agents from drug enforcement are out right now rounding the Swans up. The women too. They found enough evidence yesterday to bring them all in. I don't know if we have enough room in the cells."

They grimaced at the thought.

"Go on back. You can wait in Ben's office," Juanita said with a broad smile.

Nathan Stark sat at Ben's desk.

"I could kill Juanita," she thought as he got up to welcome her. Everyone kept trying to push them together.

"Daisy McLaren," he said. "I thought I saw you yesterday. Have a seat."

Thoughts raced through her mind so rapidly that she could not latch on to any one idea. *I've got to find Keira* alternated with *Why am I so Stupid*! Not a single thought led to an excuse to leave, so she sat.

Nathan was as attractive to her as ever. Unnerved by his proximity, she clasped her hands and made a steeple with her index fingers. She did not go as far as turning her palms out to see if the people were seated, but she welcomed this distraction of her own device.

"What you did took a lot of courage. I'm curious to know if you noticed anything along the way."

Daisy shook her head but then remembered.

"There was a road across Arrowwood. It turned to go up the mountain so I thought there could be other cabins farther up."

Nathan nodded thoughtfully.

"Do you remember where it is?"

She nodded but said, "It's not marked on any maps I have. I also looked for it last night online and couldn't find it."

"If I get some different types of maps, would you be willing to take a look?"

"Sure."

"Why don't I take you out for lunch and we can look together?"

Daisy choked and decided not to reply. She changed her tack.

"Uh, I heard the Swans are being arrested."

"Yeah, because of the meth lab. There'll be charges coming soon."

He walked over to a filing cabinet and took out a couple of folders.

"National forest service and topo maps. Let's go."

She could not think of a retort quickly enough, so simply followed him. Juanita Williams winked at Daisy as they passed her office.

She was walking toward her Jeep when Nathan called out, "Ride with me."

Quit acting like a baby with *I wish I could die right now.*

Nathan attempted to make conversation on the way over, but Daisy's thoughts muffled the sound of his voice. Questions about Jake arose. *Why am I like this around Nathan but not around Jake? Am I falling for this FBI person?*

She continued contrasting the two in her mind until they reached the restaurant.

Daisy was relieved when they pulled into the Fatz parking lot. Eleven o'clock was early lunch in Franklin, and although many locals liked to eat there because of the variety of food on the menu, it was unlikely she would see anyone she was close to. Jake only came here when she asked.

Afraid she would not be able to eat in front of Nathan, she ordered the "Loaded Baked Potato Soup." She was anxious to have done with this meal, but Nathan studied each page of the menu so carefully it seemed he would take forever. When he did decide, it was the obvious choice for the "World-Famous Calabash Fried Chicken."

Calabash is famous but not because of Fatz and not because of fried chicken. Anyone planning a vacation in Myrtle Beach knows to go to Calabash, North Carolina, for perfectly fried fish and shrimp. Ella's of Calabash was the first great seafood shack, and even it had added a landlubber's section to the menu. Unless they were allergic, everyone ordered fried, broiled, baked, or stuffed seafood.

After they had placed their orders, Nathan brought out the U.S. Forest Service map.

"This shows roads used only by the USFS agents. They maintain a system of roads, dirt and gravel, and trails to provide access for firefighting and rescue operations, if hikers get lost."

"Does it show nearby cabins?"

"Sometimes. Remote towers had what were known as cabs, either on the tower or as part of the base. The topography sometimes made it impossible, and a cabin would have to be erected nearby. Most lookout towers have been abandoned, but that's a long story."

He unfolded a large map and then carefully refolded it to show only a small area. He pointed to a spot along the Arrowwood.

"Here's where the meth lab was. Can you locate the road?"

"Here," Daisy said as she pointed to the place where a road crossed the creek. She traced along the road until she reached the symbol for a forest service lookout tower with a cabin close by.

"Can we go there? Now?"

"Hold on. I'll get with Randy Coleman, the Special Agent for the service in Franklin, and we'll check it out. You should wait in town."

"But..."

"I promise I'll tell you what we find."

Daisy was quiet as they drove back to the Sheriff's office. If there was a chance Keira could be at that cabin, and in danger, there was no way she was going to wait to find out. She thought about calling Jake to go with her but was afraid he would discourage her.

After a hasty goodbye to Nathan, she got in her Jeep and drove toward Wayah Road.

CHAPTER

54

As she approached the turn by Loafer's Glory, she noticed her fuel light was warning she needed gas. No matter that there was an official blue Gas sign on the highway, Loafer's Glory had not had active gasoline pumps in Daisy's memory nor in the memory of anyone she knew. Many a motorist was lured there by the apparently false advertising only to end up with a Coke and Nabs.

If the travelers' gas tanks were nearly empty, the store clerk could direct them to the Exxon several miles back toward Franklin on Old Murphy Road. In fact, the service station was the reason for the sign on the highway. Pity the poor traveler who depended on credit and ATM cards for payments: the Pit Stop was a cash-only pay-inside operation. If they lacked enough cash to fill the tank, they would have to buy what they could and then return to Franklin for gas. If they were wise, they would also get extra cash.

When her Jeep indicated low fuel, there was usually enough to take her another 20 to 25 miles. She made the turn onto Wayah and trusted in luck to keep her moving. She flew down the road and was almost passing by Lexie and Brad's farm when an unexpected movement caught her eye. She had driven too far down the road to see what had caused it, but she knew that the couple should be at work at the bookstore and that they did not have any hired help for the farm. She told Siri to call Lexie, who answered promptly.

"Daisy! Are you okay?"

Lexie was the sister Daisy never had, and she constantly showed her concern.

"I'm fine, but I just saw someone at your farm. I couldn't tell who it was, but they were carrying a large bundle to the stable. Have you got someone to work there?"

After a moment's silence.

"Lexie?"

"No one should be there. Brad went to get our lunch, take-out from the Gazebo, and he should be back soon. I'll get him to drive out there and see what's going on."

"I'm here now," Daisy said. "I'll take a look."

She hung up before Lexie could reply and did a Y-turn.

Daisy parked in front of the house. Since seeing Brad with Jasmine, she viewed him as a suspect. Aware of the potential for danger, she paused and considered calling Jake or her father. That would be the prudent action to take.

This is silly. It's probably just Brad coming by to get something before going back to the shop.

Still, she decided to approach the stables cautiously, in case it was someone else, someone who did not belong there. The first droplets of rain fell. Hoping to stay dry this time, she dashed across the yard and entered through the large sliding door.

Brad was nowhere to be seen. The door to the apartment was open. It had once been intended to house a groom but was now used as an office. The stalls remained empty. She walked to the door and whispered hello but got no answer.

Now she wished she had not left her iPhone in the Jeep and even more that she had thought to bring the super-sized flashlight that she purchased to do double duty as a weapon. The stable was darker than usual because of clouds bringing yet another storm to the valley. Outside thunder crashed, and lightning brightened the stalls. Having gotten her bearings, Daisy inched along to the ladder, in the center of the stable, that would take her to the hayloft.

She began to climb and was about to call out again when she heard voices arguing, she stopped. A man, certainly Brad, and a woman, certainly not Lexie who remained at the bookstore.

"I told you this was a mistake," the woman said. "We should've killed her at the cabin, like the others. Now we've got to get rid of her."

"No way," Brad said. "I didn't sign up for this. Not for murder! I haven't killed anybody yet, and I don't intend to now."

"So, you're ready to go to prison for this? You know kidnapping is a federal crime. And selling babies? They'll throw the book at you!"

"Yeah? But cold-blooded murder is life with no possibility of parole."

"Okay, then what's your bright idea? Never mind. I'll take her back with me. I know just the place for her in Atlanta."

Clasping her hand across her mouth, Daisy stepped back to the sawdust floor of the stable. She searched for a hiding place where she could gather her wits and decide what to do. Then she remembered her Jeep was parked at the house. She had to leave before they discovered it.

Thunder and lightning crashed above the farm, and the heavens opened up. She rushed to the sliding door. Pushing it out to give her just enough space to slip through, she made her escape, and the winds banged it shut behind her. Not daring to turn and look back, she raced to her Jeep and drove quickly to Wayah Road.

At last, enroute to Jake's farm, she glanced to see Brad crossing to the house with someone shrouded in a rain poncho, but she had passed by before she could see who it was.

Could Lexie know about this?

She shuddered at the thought. Danger was nearby, and she needed time to figure out what she should do.

Reaching Jake's house, she switched the ignition off and sat for a minute, taking deep breaths to ward off a panic attack that would surely incapacitate her if she allowed it. Once the fear passed, she covered her head with a new piece of folded newspaper and dashed across the yard.

CHAPTER

55

The redbone hound Susie Q was first to spy Daisy. She bounded out howling her greeting. She leapt in the air and did several pirouettes before sitting politely before her. Clemmie was rocking on the front porch with the orange tabby Ambrosia in her lap. Although Daisy was shaken by what she had just seen and heard, she did not want to alarm her or reveal anything that might cause Clemmie to act differently around Brad or Lexie. She stooped to scratch behind the hound's ears.

"Daisy, I didn't expect to see you today. What're you doing out in this weather?"

Daisy avoided the question.

"I'm sure glad you're home. I thought the storm wouldn't get here until later. Is Jake around?"

"No, but he should be here soon. Why don't you stay and eat with us? I'm about to give the baby a bottle. You could feed her if you want."

"I wish I could, but I can't today. Can you ask him to call me when he gets in?"

"Of course, dear, but you're welcome to wait."

"I've got to get back. To Dad. I better go now."

Not giving Clemmie time to object, she covered her head again with the folded paper and ran to her Jeep. She did not leave immediately but sat to think about what she should do. She fretted about Lexie. *No way was Lexie a part of this, but what if she were?* If Daisy warned her, she might well be warning Brad and his accomplice too. They might decide to kill their captive who Daisy felt sure was Keira. She actually hoped it *was* Keira because that would mean she was alive.

"Where is Jake when I need him?" she said aloud. Instead of calling him herself, she rationalized that Clemmie would give him her message. She called the sheriff's office where Juanita Williams answered the phone.

"Is Ben there? This is Daisy."

"No, he's not. He's out with the DEA rounding up the Swans."

"Darn it!" Daisy said. "Please tell him that I think Brad is holding Keira at his stable. They might be moving her so I'm going back to see if I can help her."

"Daisy, no!" Juanita said to a dial tone. Once again Daisy had hung up before anyone could tell her to stop and wait. So close to finding Keira, time was of the essence.

She pulled out onto Wayah Road and drove to a spot close to, but out of sight of, Lexie and Brad's place. She unlocked the glove compartment and took out the Sig Sauer handgun that Jake helped her buy and taught her how to use, and her Stinger flashlight that could also be used as a weapon. Putting her phone in her pocket, she walked carefully close to the edge of the road where a green mantle of kudzu had overtaken the shrubbery and weeds.

When she reached the beginning of the property, she stopped to inspect the magazine and make sure it was fully loaded. She turned the safety off and chambered a round. Just as she was stepping into the yard, she heard the front door opening and Brad saying, "I'll take you to get your car, and then I've got to get back to the store or Lexie will worry."

Daisy halted.

She could see Brad and then, following close behind, the woman she had seen with him and Jasmine in town. With no time to think, she took out her gun and stepped into the clearing.

"Freeze!" she shouted as she had heard police do on TV.

Brad stopped, but the woman aimed her weapon and fired in reply to Daisy, who squeezed the trigger as she fell back into the kudzu.

Grateful that she was not wounded, she winced at her own stupidity. Finding the courage to take another look, she saw Brad on the ground and no sign of the woman.

Out of nowhere sirens wailed and lights flashed as help arrived from all quarters at once. Law enforcement vehicles, fire engines, and ambulances filled the yard. Motors groaned in neutral gears, and lights flashed blue and red.

Daisy searched the crowd until she spotted Jake.

Catching his eye, she waved him toward the stables as she ran to meet him at the large sliding door.

"Keira?" he asked.

"I think she's in the loft."

Daisy paused to bend over and hold her stomach.

"Are you all right?"

"I don't know. I'm so afraid of what we'll find. I'm afraid for Keira."

She grasped Jake's arm.

"Brad? Is he dead?"

"Not sure. I don't think so."

He slid the door half open, and they slipped inside. He closed the door behind them to shut out the commotion, lights, and crowd noises. The thick door and rain that was still pouring down muffled those sounds. The eerie, dark silence of the barn frightened Daisy.

"Do you want to wait while I look?"

She shook her head.

"I've come this far. The ladder's over here."

She reached up to grab the sides of the ladder and stepped slowly on each rung to climb.

"Hello," she whispered, "Keira, are you there?"

The only answer was a low moaning, a good sound to Daisy's ears as it meant that whoever was in the hayloft was still alive. She hurried up the last rungs of the ladder with Jake close behind.

Bales of hay, harvested into cubes, were in stacked the loft. Leaning against one was Keira, groggy but alive. The other woman was not to be seen.

"Thank God," Daisy said as she went to kneel beside her. Jake soon followed.

Daisy cried tears of relief as she knelt to hug Keira. "You're okay now. I've got you."

Jake said, "I'll get help. I don't think we should move her."

Daisy nodded and, still weeping, smoothed Keira's brow and hair. Both she and Keira were crying.

"How did you find me? I thought she was going to kill me," she bawled.

"You couldn't have thought we'd forget about you?"

"My baby?"

"Needs her mother. Clemmie has been looking after her."

CHAPTER

56

Once Keira was in an ambulance, and activity at the scene was geared toward gathering evidence and roping off the scene, Daisy said to Jake, "We need to look for that woman, and I'm sure Jasmine is involved in this."

"We don't need to look for anyone. That's Ben's job."

Daisy knew that, logically, he made sense, but her gut told her otherwise.

"Look, at least let's go check on Retta. I don't think Jasmine would let anyone hurt her, but I don't want her to learn what's happened from the news."

"There's also Lexie," Jake pointed out. "She needs to know about Brad."

Daisy felt like crying.

"Do you think she was a part of this?"

"There's one way to find out."

"I'm going straight to see Retta. Can you get Lexie and bring her there?"

Daisy tried to imagine what she could say to Retta, how to approach her with the news that she thought Jasmine had helped kidnap Keira. Had she not seen Jasmine with both Brad and the mysterious woman, she would not believe it herself.

Before she had time to plan what to say, she was at Retta's cabin. Unsure of what she would find, she knocked on the door. Louisa soon opened it and shooed her back to the kitchen saying, "You're just in time. We got field peas and corn bread..." She stopped mid-sentence when she saw Daisy's expression.

"Lordy, come sit down."

"Has Jasmine been here?"

Louisa shook her head.

"You both better sit down."

Mumbling to herself, Louisa led the way to the kitchen where Retta was busy at the stove.

"What's wrong, dear? You look like you've seen a ghost. Are Clemmie and the baby all right?"

Daisy nodded and once they were all seated at the kitchen table, she described the morning's events, ending with, "Jasmine might be involved."

Louisa exclaimed, "No," but Retta just nodded her head.

"Why?"

"I've seen her with this woman and Brad. I don't know who the woman is, but she wanted to kill Keira."

"Lordy."

"That's enough, Louisa." Retta shushed her. "I figured she was up to something when she didn't come see us. I never thought..."

When Jake arrived with Lexie, Retta took over.

"Let's get you a warm bath and clean clothes to put on, dear," she said as she shepherded Lexie to a bedroom.

Jake said, "She didn't know anything. I think she's in shock, but she refused to go to the hospital. She didn't want to see Brad. How're you doing?"

In answer Daisy hugged him tightly.

"I don't know what I would've done if you hadn't been there."

Trying to make light of it, Jake laughed.

"Well, darlin', next time you might try calling me before you go off half-cocked."

"Well, isn't this cozy?"

Jake looked over Daisy's head to see Jasmine smirking in the doorway.

"Speak of the devil!"

Daisy's jaw dropped when she saw who he was referring to.

"I've been called a lot of things, but this is a new one."

She looked Daisy and Jake up and down.

"I always wondered when you two would actually get together. Am I getting an invite to the wedding?"

Daisy reckoned she had been getting good at ignoring people, so she did not answer but instead offered, "You've got a lot of nerve showing your face here. We just told your mother what you and Brad had been up to. Not to mention that stranger. How about telling us who she is and, more importantly, where she is now?"

"I wish I knew what you're talking about. Where's my mother?"

"Not so fast"

She took a moment to look Jasmine up and down. Always pretty, in her early thirties she had matured into a beautiful woman by anyone's standards. *Had Brad found her irresistible*? Even now Daisy could not help comparing herself to Jasmine, and as usual in her mind Jasmine won. Always better-looking, better at cheering, but, when Daisy thought about her new relationship with Jake, she knew she had come out ahead in the most important area. It had taken her years to see what Jasmine had seen at Franklin High.

"I don't think Brad thought up this scheme all by himself."

Jasmine regarded her with wonder.

"What 'scheme' are you talking about?"

"Don't act like you don't know."

"Daisy, I really don't have the faintest idea what you're talking about."

Determined not to let Jasmine get away with kidnapping Keira, she said, "I saw you with Brad at the bookstore. You didn't buy any books, so what were you doing there? Brad was home with Lexie when Keira was abducted, so he couldn't have taken her. Was it you?"

Jasmine dropped her eyes. When she looked at Daisy again, she said, "It's been over for quite a while. Since you insist on knowing, Brad and I were sleeping together."

"Seriously! You expect me to believe that?"

Now looking at Jasmine's face, she knew it was true. It

took a moment to recover and attack again.

"Well, who was that woman I saw you with?"

"What woman?"

"Don't try to act innocent. The woman at the BP. She was in a silver truck. I saw you talking to her."

"Oh, her."

"Yes, her. Brad was helping her hide Keira in his stables."

"I met her once when Brad came to see me in Atlanta. Brad said she was his cousin. I think he said her name was Frances, Fran Robbins. That's it. I never saw her again. Maybe Brad can tell you more."

Daisy had no comeback for that except for one last question.

"So, what are you doing in Franklin? You weren't visiting Retta until today."

"It's not really any of your business, but I've bought a house in Franklin. I've come to tell my mother, so if you don't mind..."

As she walked off, Jake looked askance at Daisy.

"I don't even want to know what you're thinking, but whatever it is, don't do it. I'm going to carry Mama and the baby to the hospital so Keira can see her baby when she wakes up."

"I'll be right behind you," Daisy fudged the truth. "I forgot to ask Retta something."

Jake hesitated but then kissed her. As usual, he knew better than to attempt to stop her.

"See you at the hospital."

CHAPTER

57

Jasmine moving to Franklin meant only one thing for Daisy: trouble.

Living in Jasmine's shadow had been hard enough at Franklin High, but now? Just when everything was starting to go so well in her personal life.

She followed Jasmine back into the cabin. When she reached the kitchen, the stunned look on Retta's face said that Jasmine had already dropped her bomb. The news had momentarily struck Louisa dumb, but she was fast recovering and was already reaching out to smother Jasmine in her embrace.

Retta snapped at Louisa.

"For heaven's sake, Louisa. Let Jasmine be."

Daisy sat at the table as Retta continued. "It's not that I don't want you here, Jasmine dear, but what about your job? Your life in Atlanta?"

"Well, most of my work now is online, and I can do that anywhere. I found the perfect house, and you know it just was the right time."

"I see. Where is the house?"

"It's in Laurel Ridge. Near the top. It's got wonderful views. I can't wait for you to see it."

Daisy knew all about Laurel Ridge, a small community with about 80 houses built to take advantage of the mountain slopes. Most had two stories with a basement-level garage. The entrance was directly across from Jake's farm and just down the road from Brad and Lexie. If she moved to live with Jake in the house he was building, Jasmine would be her neighbor.

Daisy had been mute, but now said, "Why? Why now?"

The look on Jasmine's face said that she thought the question was ridiculous.

"Why?" she said. "To be near my mother. And Louisa, of course."

Having heard Jasmine deliver many a backhanded compliment at Franklin High and at UNC, she knew she could be insincere. She never thought she would subject Retta to her deceptions.

"Oh Lordy, we got to celebrate." Louisa burst into the conversation as was her wont. "I got some cookies I made this morning."

"I can't stay. I have to arrange for the movers to come, and I'm meeting with a contractor about renovations for the place. We can really celebrate after I move."

Daisy broke in.

"Brad's in the hospital."

Unblinking, Jasmine looked her straight in the eye and

said, "Oh no. What's wrong with him?"

As Louisa went on and on about Keira, Brad, and Lexie, Daisy kept her eyes fixed on Jasmine. She shivered at the certainty that Jasmine not only already knew about Brad but also knew about everything else.

"Keira Swan is there too, in the hospital. I'm going to see her now."

"Oh?"

"She should be able to tell us what happened to her."

Jasmine shrugged.

"Well, that'll be great. It's so scary to hear about kidnappings and gun fights in Franklin. I hope all that's in the past. I was just up there, to sign up for volunteering. I'd have stopped by to see them if I'd known."

Daisy almost laughed at the thought of Jasmine as a candy-striper but remembered all the things she did to look good for her admissions applications to college. *Could she actually be innocent*? *Could I just be hoping to find a flaw in Jasmine's seeming perfection*?

"I'm sure they would've appreciated a visit. Especially Brad. I'm going now and will let them know."

"Don't rush off on my account."

"I was on the way out."

She hugged Retta and Louisa and air-kissed Jasmine.

"We can catch up later."

As Daisy backed out to return to Franklin, she realized that during the day the sun had come out. Now the cool evening air was creating a heavy fog to shroud the forest and its laurel undergrowth with a dark cloak. A dense mist painted the trees and thickets black and obscured the dirt and gravel road.

She had rescued Keira but was no closer to discovering who had killed her mother. Alice McLaren was lured to her death by a woman promising information, but she would never have met someone she did not know, especially in such an isolated area. Millicent Jordan had revealed that her mother was meeting a woman. Frances Robbins? Maybe Brad could tell her.

What was the weather like when Mom died? Could it have just been an accident in weather like this? If she were murdered, could Brad have done it? He claimed he'd never killed, but...

The Jeep jerked in and out of a deep groove in the road.

She crept along until she reached the parking lot for the ER at the hospital. Her cell chimed as she got out.

"Daisy."

"I'm here, Jake. I swear. I'm in the parking lot now."

"It's not that, darlin'. Brad died before I got here. Mama and the baby are with Keira, and they're okay."

Jake was silent as Daisy absorbed what he was telling her.

"Why am I getting a bad feeling?"

"It's Lucas."

Daisy's throat clutched as she held her breath.

"He's here. As a patient. Come to the ICU."

"Why, Jake? Just tell me now."

"Lucas has had a stroke."

Acknowledgements

Many thanks to my family and friends who encourage me to continue telling the story of Daisy and Jake. They have faith in the story even as I feel I'm telling it poorly. The toughest critic of writing is the writer herself. My sister Mary and my friend Jane were the steadiest voices.

Virtual writing groups, especially the London Writers Salon at 8 a.m. and the #5amwritersclub on Twitter, kept me on track to write and revise daily.

Thanks to The Book Khaleesi for having my back with technical publishing issues and for producing a professional product.

Finally, a huge thank you to all the other writers who publish independently. As they win major awards and attract readers, they gain our books acceptance in the broader community.

About the Author

Ruth McCoy is the pen name of Linda McCoy Cromartie. Growing up in Mississippi, she left to study English in North Carolina. Since graduation, she has lived in Washington DC, Northern Virginia, another stint in Chapel Hill, Athens GA, and back again in North Carolina — this time in the small mountain town of Franklin. The rich history, legends, and natural environment of the high valley town and surrounding mountains continually inspire her writing.

Made in the USA
Columbia, SC
01 June 2023

17588285R00143